With Valentine's Day, February is always a romantic month. And we've got some great books in store for you....

The High-Society Wife by Helen Bianchin is the story of a marriage of convenience between two rich and powerful families.... But what this couple didn't expect is for their marriage to become real! It's also the first in our new miniseries RUTHLESS, where you'll find commanding men, who stop at nothing to get what they want. Look out for more books coming soon! And if you love Italian men, don't miss *The Marchese's Love-Child* by Sara Craven, where our heroine is swept off her feet by a passionate tycoon.

If you just want to get away from it all, let us whisk you off to the beautiful Greek Islands in Julia James's hard-hitting story *Baby of Shame*. What will happen when a businessman discovers that his night of passion with a young Englishwoman five years ago resulted in a son? The Caribbean is the destination for our couple in Anne Mather's intriguing tale *The Virgin's Seduction*.

Jane Porter has a dangerously sexy Sicilian for you in *The Sicilian's Defiant Mistress*. This explosive reunion story promises to be dark and passionate! In Trish Morey's *Stolen by the Sheikh,* the first in her new duet, THE ARRANGED BRIDES, a young woman is summoned to the palace of a demanding sheikh, who has plans for her future.... Don't miss part two, coming in March.

See the inside front cover for a list of titles and book numbers.

Dear Reader,

Sapphy is an up-and-coming fashion designer based in Milan, and she's been badgering me to tell her story. But the closer I looked, the more it became apparent that there were two stories to tell, each featuring a strong alpha hero and bound together by a secret wedding and the burning need for revenge. Thus THE ARRANGED BRIDES duet was born.

Stolen by the Sheikh tells Sapphy's story: how she meets up with Sheikh Khaled Al-Ateeq, a ruthless man more than prepared to use her to settle a score with his old enemy, Paolo. But in the process he loses his heart to Sapphy, only to find he ultimately wins something much more satisfying than revenge—her love!

What happens when Paolo learns that the sheikh has exacted his revenge as he had always promised he would? Watch out for my upcoming title, *The Mancini Marriage Bargain* next month and find out.

I hope you enjoy reading THE ARRANGED BRIDES stories as much as I enjoyed writing them. If you'd like to learn more about me or my books, visit my Web site at www.trishmorey.com and maybe even drop me a line. I love hearing from readers.

Happy reading!

Trish x

Trish Morey

STOLEN BY THE SHEIKH

The Arranged Brides

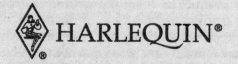

HARLEQUIN®

TORONTO • NEW YORK • LONDON
AMSTERDAM • PARIS • SYDNEY • HAMBURG
STOCKHOLM • ATHENS • TOKYO • MILAN • MADRID
PRAGUE • WARSAW • BUDAPEST • AUCKLAND

ISBN 0-373-12522-4

STOLEN BY THE SHEIKH

First North American Publication 2006.

www.eHarlequin.com

Printed in U.S.A.

All about the author...
Trish Morey

TRISH MOREY wrote her first book at age eleven
for a children's book-week competition; entitled
Island Dreamer, it proved to be her first rejection.
Shattered and broken, she turned to a life where she
could combine her love of fiction with her need
for creativity—and became a chartered accountant.
Life wasn't all dull though, as she embarked on a
skydiving course, completing three jumps before
deciding that she'd given her fear of heights a run
for its money.

Meanwhile, she fell in love and married a handsome
guy who cut computer code. After the birth of their
second daughter, Trish spied an article saying that
Harlequin® was actively seeking new authors. It was
one of those eureka moments—Trish was going to be
one of those authors!

Eleven years after reading that fateful article, the
magical phone call came and Trish finally realized her
dream. According to Trish, writing and selling a book
is a major life achievement that ranks right up there
with jumping out of an airplane and motherhood.
All three take commitment, determination and sheer
guts, but the effort is so very, very worthwhile.

Trish now lives with her husband and four young
daughters in a special part of south Australia,
surrounded by orchards and bushland and visited
by the occasional koala and kangaroo.

You can visit Trish at her Web site at
www.trishmorey.com or drop her a line at
trish@trishmorey.com.

CHAPTER ONE

SHE knew it without turning.

The sudden flush to her skin, the disconcerting prickle that crawled the length of her spine, told Sapphy Clemenger that whoever had just entered Bacelli's Milan salon was no ordinary customer. In an atmosphere that suddenly felt superheated, instinct screamed that no way was this one of her usual clients rushing in five minutes before evening closing time to search for the perfect outfit to woo her husband, or even her lover.

Her muscles strained and tensed, her senses heightening so much that even the hushed click of the cushioned door closing registered to her senses as significant.

Battling the sensations that continued to skitter up and down her back, she blinked away the weariness bequeathed by her 3 a.m. mornings leading up to this week's successful fashion-week show and swivelled right, a smile of welcome at the ready, only to have her eyes jag on blackness.

His power hit her first.

Like a rush of electricity she felt his impact surge over her. He was a wall of power, a wall of authority. Black roll-neck sweater, well-cut black jeans topping hand-stitched black boots. Even his hair glossed blue-black in the beam from the ceiling's downlights.

But it was his eyes that reached across the room and snared her. Dark and fathomless with a glint that came and went like a shooting star in the night sky, their midnight quality reeled her in.

Was it possible to feel your pupils dilate? *Yes*, if what she'd just experienced was any indication. And given the sensory heights she seemed to be suddenly subjected to in the last few seconds, maybe she shouldn't be surprised.

He said nothing as he moved towards her, never taking his eyes from her face and leaving no doubt in her mind that he hadn't just stumbled upon the salon.

He'd come to see her.

She shivered, instantly regretting letting Carla, the salon's permanent assistant, go home early. This was no time to be alone. But still she didn't move. Not that she was certain she could. It was all she could do to swallow as he devoured the distance between them.

'Buona sera,' he said, his voice rich and deep and containing so many influences she couldn't place his accent. 'Or would you prefer I speak English?'

His lips curved slightly yet lacked any real warmth in a face that seemed all harsh angles and planes. She felt her eyes narrow. So he knew she wasn't Italian. What else did he know about her? *And why?*

'Thank you. English will be fine.' Her voice sounded remarkably steadier than she felt as she readily accepted his offer to use her native tongue. After four years working in Italy away from her Australian homeland, she spoke fluent Italian, but here, in this man's presence, she didn't trust herself to think and speak her adopted language without tripping over her tongue. 'How can I help you?'

'You are, I presume, Sapphire Clemenger? The designer?'

Still she couldn't place his accent. It held touches of English, a trace of American and more besides. He wasn't Italian, of that she was sure, even though his dark features could have passed for Mediterranean. Yet he was too tall, too broad in the shoulders.

And much, much too close.

The heat came off him in waves. She felt herself flush, her mouth desert dry. Finally she nodded in answer to his question, incapable of forming the words.

'I suspected as much,' he continued. 'I understood you to be quite beautiful. Of course, until now I had no idea just how much.'

She blinked slowly as something lurched inside her. How could just a few words affect her so deeply? She was used to the flattery and attention she received from the local males. They had a reputation for appreciating the feminine form and they certainly lived up to it. But it was always given in good spirit and in a way that was more lighthearted than serious.

This man's words resonated on another level entirely. Maybe it was something to do with the way his eyes continued to scrutinise her face as if drinking in every detail, to rake over her body with the hot power of a blowtorch.

And still she didn't know who he was.

She straightened her back, pushing herself taller and battling to damp down her own mounting temperature. She'd had enough of being on the defensive.

'You seem to have me at a disadvantage, Signor…?'

'Call me Khaled,' he said, offering her his hand.

She took it and almost immediately wished she hadn't, sensing her new-found courage melt away. For now, with his long, tapered fingers enclosing hers, their latent strength seeping into her flesh, she felt as if he'd somehow taken charge, as if he somehow possessed her.

And that was crazy.

She didn't belong to anyone, least of all to this dark stranger. Even Paolo, whom she'd been seeing on and off for more than two years, didn't instil this sense of possession in her.

She tugged on her hand, aware the stranger had been holding on to it for much too long, and stepped around him, focusing on steadying the rhythm of her breathing as she headed for the salon's lounge area. *If she didn't have to concentrate on standing up, maybe she could think more clearly.* She indicated an armchair while she glanced over to the door, willing someone, *anyone,* to enter the store. 'Please,' she said over her shoulder, 'tell me how I can help you.'

He watched her panicked retreat and her longing glance at the passing pedestrians with some entertainment. He'd been right to wait until now to make his move. It was late and unlikely anyone else would visit the salon and interrupt them. Unlikely anyone would come to her rescue.

She turned and looked at him, the questions laid bare in her large blue eyes. He could see her vulnerability and how she was fighting it. He could feel her suspicion, warring with curiosity.

He could taste her fear.

She was much more interesting than he'd been led to believe. And more beautiful. Even with tell-tale smudges of tiredness around her eyes, they shone with life and promise in features arranged perfectly on her face. Her dark-gold hair was swept up into a sleek curve that exposed the smooth sweep of her neck.

The face of a model and the body of a goddess. Paolo couldn't have chosen better.

She would do perfectly.

'What can I do for you, Signor Khaled?' she asked as he curved his length into the plush Venetian-style chair opposite her own. 'Are you looking for something for a special woman?'

He smiled, more to himself than outwardly. 'You could say that. Your designs are the talk of Milan. Your show was an outstanding success. For a foreigner you have done remarkably well in breaking into such a competitive market.'

'I've been very lucky.'

'You are very talented,' he said. 'Otherwise you would not be where you are.'

'Thank you,' she said quietly, her cheeks surprisingly tinged with pink, almost as if she was unused to compliments. 'Was there something in the collection that particularly interested you?'

'It is all of interest. But that's not why I'm here. I want you to make a dress.'

He saw the interest flare in her eyes. 'Certainly. That's not a problem. I do commission work for many of my clients.'

He could see by her body language that she was finally relaxing as they spoke, back in the familiar territory of what she did best. Her shoulders looked less rigid and, by the steady rise and fall of her chest, her breathing appeared more under control. She assumed he was just one more customer. This would be almost too easy.

'This will be no ordinary dress,' he continued. 'I am to be married in four weeks. I want you to design and construct a wedding gown for my wife-to-be.'

A wedding dress. She loved all of her design work but always the greatest satisfaction, the greatest thrill, came in designing wedding gowns, a woman's most important dress for her most important day. A dress that complemented, that accentuated while it minimised and made the most of the bride as it transformed her into a princess; Sapphy loved nothing more than to make it happen. But he was cutting it fine.

'A wedding gown in just four weeks? Usually we would recommend at least three times that for something so special.'

'With your talent, I should not think that will be a problem.'

Her pulse raced at the opportunity he was offering while her mind was busy negotiating the difficulties that still stood in the way of accepting the job. 'Thank you. You pay me a huge compliment by even offering me this commission. However, as much as I am tempted, I do have other responsibilities and other clients I must consider before I can accept.'

He pushed himself from the chair and loomed over her. 'But you have just shown your latest collection. That is completed. You *will* design this dress.'

She felt her eyes widen, taken aback as much at his physical presence before her as his bold statement. Until now he'd given the impression he specifically wanted her to design the wedding gown. Could it be that other designers had already turned down the commission? Maybe desperation was forcing his hand and he'd run out of options.

Besides, as tempted as she was to take on any wedding-gown design project, she would be mad to promise something she could not deliver. Especially just because it was demanded of her. 'I'm still not a free agent. I do have my own line now, it's true, but I still work within the House of Bacelli.'

'I have already spoken with Gianfranco Bacelli. He will release you.'

'I see.' But she didn't see. She bit down on her lip as she considered his revelation. This was no ordinary commission, not if it had already been squared away with the ageing designer who headed the Bacelli house. Whoever this Khaled was, he was a man of influence. And he obviously expected her to fall in with his plans.

He took a step closer. 'You will be compensated well.'

She stood up, forcing her five-feet-eight frame taller, wanting to show him she would not be the pushover he expected, though she still conceded a good six inches to his height. 'Be that as it may, you have left things very late. As you are no doubt aware, I work to the highest possible standards and that means it may simply not be feasible to do the dress justice in the time available.'

'Name your price, then.'

She drew back, offended by the implication. 'Signor Khaled, you misunderstand me. I wasn't angling at securing a higher price for my services, merely pointing out that the time is very short even to complete the design to the satisfaction of the bride, let alone to construct the dress.'

He waved away her umbrage with a flick of his wrist, almost as if he was bored. 'This dress will be your design. You are the designer.'

'But surely the bride will want to have her say? Perhaps she'd like to come in, we can talk about it together, get some ideas down on paper?'

'No!' He glowered down at her. 'That will not be possible.' He turned and strode to the window. 'She knows your designs. She would have no one else design her wedding dress. You will design it yourself.'

She shook her head. 'I'm afraid that makes the job

almost impossible, then. At a minimum I need to know the bride's tastes and preferences. I need to know what colours best suit her and what styles complement her figure.'

'You cannot meet her. At least—not yet.'

'But why? What bride doesn't want to be involved in organising her own gown?'

His dark eyes narrowed. 'She is…indisposed. The wedding will be challenge enough for her. She doesn't need the additional stress beforehand.'

'Oh, I see.' Sapphy's mind whirled with the possibilities. What could be the problem? Unless she was ill, too ill to handle her own wedding plans. That might also explain the rush…

Her heart filled with compassion. It all fitted. His bride was ill, perhaps seriously, and they wanted to marry while they still could. No wonder he was so desperate to retain her services. No wonder he seemed so angry with her.

'I can tell you all you need to know,' he said. 'I can answer all your questions. So, will you design the gown?'

She swallowed, trying to ease the sudden constriction in her throat. If she was right about the circumstances of this marriage, there was no way she couldn't help. There was no way she could let a bride in such circumstances down. But likewise she wanted more than anything for the bride to be delighted with her dress and, without the usual input, how could she be sure she could pull it off?

'This is a heavy responsibility. I would need to be

sure the bride will be satisfied with the gown. I would hate for her to be disappointed in any way.'

'I guarantee, she will love it.' He suddenly pivoted to face her, as if something had occurred to him. 'All she asks...'

Sapphy's ears pricked up, eager for anything that would give her some indication of the bride's preferences. 'Yes?'

He smiled, his teeth white against his tanned skin and his eyes shining in the glow from the downlights. 'All she asks is that you imagine that this is your wedding, that you imagine you are the bride and that this is the gown of your dreams. Only then will she be happy.'

Her eyelids fell shut, long and purposefully, as the tingles she'd thought long gone resumed their samba along her spine. A client was paying her the ultimate compliment, letting her decide everything about the dress's style, fabric and design. It was an unbelievable opportunity to showcase her talent. Yet something still didn't feel right.

And part of it was in imagining this was her wedding and the resultant picture that flashed through her mind's eye. She was walking down the carpeted aisle towards the man waiting for her. But something was wrong. The man was wrong.

It wasn't Paolo waiting for her.

It was Signor Khaled.

She shuddered and forced her eyes open, staring out into the busy Via Monte Napoleone in an effort to banish the unwelcome pictures from her mind.

He was nothing to her. Nothing but another client and one who was marrying another woman—a sick woman if the indications were correct. So why would she imagine even for a second the thought of marrying such a man? And why did the images persist?

She had to focus on the bride and her gown. This would be her day and Sapphy would do all she could to make it the most special day in the world for her. 'I'll still need to meet her at some stage, of course,' she said, turning away from the traffic at last. 'I'll need to do at least some fittings.'

'We will deal with that in Jebbai. I have organised a studio for you. You can start work as soon as you arrive.'

'In Jebbai?' Warning bells rang loud in her mind. 'But that's somewhere out in the desert. You expect me to go there?'

'Jebbai is an independent state. You have no need to fear. You will be safe while you are in my care. I guarantee that.'

'But why can't I do the job here? I have clients who will need me, I have access to all the fabrics...'

'Gianfranco Bacelli has taken care of all that.' He smiled, or was it just the way he tilted his head? 'And you do want to meet the bride, don't you?'

She paused, licked her dry lips. 'I still haven't agreed to do this.'

'No?' he asked, as if he believed she had no choice. 'Then you have until Sunday to decide. We fly out Monday.'

CHAPTER TWO

SAPPHY let herself into her apartment, tired but at the same time exhilarated. While her body was tingling from her unexpected meeting with Signor Khaled, her mind was weighed down with uncertainty.

The proposal had come completely out of the blue, but given that her current collection and the shows were complete, the timing really couldn't be better. Nevertheless, it would still be tight, designing and completing something special within four weeks.

If she agreed to go to Jebbai.

Jebbai.

Just the name was enough to conjure up exotic images of endless golden sand and swaying palm trees. But what did she really know about the desert kingdom other than that it was a small independent Arab state, landlocked by sand and that it had made its fortune with its rich oil reserves?

She flicked through her small pile of mail, finding nothing there compelling enough to open immediately and distract her thoughts, so she put the letters back down and moved to the glass doors overlooking her small balcony. She stepped out into the cool air, leaning her forearms on the railing, watching the people in the square below enjoying the surprisingly mild February evening, milling about talking to friends or

18

drifting off to one of the restaurants lining the small square.

The commission was tempting, the location alluring, but there was something wholly unsettling about the man, something intangible that seemed to reach out and grab hold of her.

It wasn't just his sultry dark looks, though now at last they were explained. She could see the Arab influence in his features and his bearing and even in the golden glow to his skin. As if he was made for the desert.

In normal circumstances his looks would have been enough to get him noticed, though they were hardly unsettling. What rattled her more was his brooding presence and the way his whole attitude spoke of thinly veiled contempt.

Why should he be angry with her? Unless he was driven by desperation to obtain the services of a designer in time for his wedding and her failure to immediately acquiesce to his demands had displeased him. No, thinking back, he'd seemed angry even when he entered the salon.

Angry and demanding.

Did she really want to fly off to some desert state with him? Did she want to be trapped with him in a vessel as small as a plane? He'd burned up the atmosphere in the salon. Sucked the air dry. Even a plane as large as a seven-four-seven would be hard-pressed to hold enough oxygen for them both.

As much as she was tempted by the commission, by the chance to experience the desert and of designing a wedding dress like nothing she'd ever done before, she certainly wasn't keen on spending another moment in Signor Khaled's company.

She hugged her arms to her, the night's chill finally registering, and stepped back inside, pulling the doors shut behind her. Out of the corner of her eye, she noticed a tiny flashing light. A message on her answer machine; maybe Paolo had called...

She punched the play button but it was Gianfranco's gravelly tones that filled the room. 'Expect a new client,' he said in his rich Italian voice. 'This will be very good for your profile and for the House of Bacelli. I expect you to take this commission.'

The machine beeped its conclusion as nerve endings tingled. There was no getting out of it now. She wasn't fooled by Gianfranco's use of language. What Gianfranco 'expected', invariably happened. So where did that leave her now?

Most likely on a plane to Jebbai on Monday.

Which meant the one thing she didn't want to deal with. She shivered. She wouldn't be travelling alone.

Signor Khaled would be on the plane with her.

She wandered around the living area, retrieving the pile of mail and slapping it firmly against her hand, jolting herself back to reality.

What the hell was wrong with her? As if she'd have to spend time with him once they arrived in Jebbai. He was obviously a person of some wealth to be able to employ at such short notice one of Milan's upcoming designers from one of its leading houses. And he was setting her up in a workshop so she could perform her duties. Clearly he wanted her to complete the gown as soon as possible so that he could marry his fiancée, no doubt during which he had other more pressing duties to attend to.

There was little risk she wouldn't be able to complete the dress in time. While the four-week timetable would be tight, being relieved of her other workload and able to work on the dress full-time made meeting his deadline that much more achievable.

And hadn't she secretly been attracted to the idea of visiting the desert state? Maybe a visit to Jebbai was just what she needed to infuse some fresh ideas into her designs.

Already she could imagine the light of the desert land—the sun would be bright, perhaps even more bold than the harsh sun she knew back in Australia, but she wanted to experience its heat, she wanted to see its dipping rays burn the desert sands red. Colours in Jebbai would seem more intense, fabrics sheer and silky and lush with embroidery.

There would be different fragrances, different textures and sensations. She'd be crazy to miss out on such an experience, surely.

She looked around back into her modest apartment. Her modest, *lonely* apartment. There was nothing holding her here. Even Paolo was still in the States, working on a complex international lawsuit. A case likely to take months by the sounds of it.

Meanwhile she could be exploring a new part of the world. It would almost be like a holiday.

Goodness, after the hours she put in for Gianfranco, she could do with one of those.

Halfway through her opening her neglected mail the doorbell rang. Her insides lurched on a reflex.

Signor Khaled!

But it couldn't be. He didn't even know where she lived. Although from what she'd seen of him to date, a mere technicality like that was hardly likely to stand in his way.

She made her way to the door, heart pumping in anticipation of once again seeing one person who had so dominated her thoughts since their meeting. Tentatively she pulled open the door, only to be pulled into the arms of the man waiting on the other side.

'Sapphy, bella!'

'Paolo?' Trepidation melted into surprise as she found herself being pulled into a firm embrace and on the receiving end of a kiss. 'I didn't expect to see you.'

He relaxed his grip, holding her away a fraction and looking down at her curiously. 'What's wrong— aren't you pleased to see me?'

She laughed, apprehension turning to relief as she stood in the arms of the good-looking Italian, and she hugged him in return. 'Of course I am. I've missed you. It's just that it's such a surprise—a nice surprise. Come in.'

He followed her into the apartment as she hit him with a barrage of questions—*When did you get back? How long can you stay? Has the case finished?*

'Enough,' he said with a smile, holding up one hand as he accepted with the other the glass of wine she'd poured as her questions continued to spill out. 'The case is in recess while the defence prepares to introduce some new evidence. I don't have long, it was just too good an opportunity not to visit, seeing I missed your show. I hear you were a great success.'

She looked up at him and swallowed the disappointment he'd just awakened. He hadn't made it to her show, hadn't been with her on the most successful night of her career. And while she'd known there was little chance he'd make it, part of her knew that at one time in their relationship he would have moved heaven and earth to be there.

'After not seeing you for six weeks, I'm just glad you're here now,' she said honestly, curling into him on the sofa and breathing in his familiar cologne. 'We haven't had much time together lately.'

She sipped from her own glass and knew that in her tired state she'd soon need some food to counteract the wine or she'd be asleep in minutes. 'Are you hungry? Would you like to go out somewhere for dinner?'

'No,' he said, almost too quickly. Then he gave her shoulders a squeeze. 'It's been a long day and I have to head to the Villa tomorrow to see my family before I fly back to the States. So why don't we have dinner here, have a quiet night? What do you think?'

Sapphy nodded and settled into the curve of his arm. It was just so good to see him again, she'd eat anywhere.

And even if he wasn't jet lagged, she'd half expected his response. In the weeks prior to his departure for New York, it seemed everywhere the couple had gone together they'd been besieged by the paparazzi, anxious to find a match between the famous international lawyer and the upcoming fashion designer. She'd lost count of the number of articles citing her as the 'imminent Signora Mancini'.

The articles didn't bother her overly much but they'd obviously had a different effect on Paolo. When she'd jokingly asked Paolo if he could take a hint, his reaction had been to withdraw from public life altogether and from her almost as much. She'd seen less and less of him, until finally he'd announced he was handling the New York case himself and had disappeared for who knew how long.

But he was here now. She put down her glass and let go a breath, feeling the tension from the day disappearing as she relaxed back into him again.

'Difficult day?' he asked.

She considered her response, his adjective immediately bringing to mind the salon's final visitor. 'Um, it was long. And interesting. Actually it's lucky you dropped by this weekend. It looks like I'm going away for a few weeks to work on commission for a new client.'

'Sounds interesting.'

'Gianfranco is pushing me. He says it will be good for my career. And, of course, for the House of Bacelli. I'm to design a wedding gown. Should be away four weeks.'

'Where are you going?'

'Somewhere out in the desert. A place called Jebbai.'

She heard the breath hiss through his teeth, felt his muscles tense beneath her, so tight it was almost as if he'd turned to stone.

'Sapphy,' he said, his voice barely more than a husky whisper and with a note that immediately alerted her. 'What's the name of your new client?'

She laughed nervously. 'Why? What's wrong?'

'Tell me!'

Her laughter dried up and she swallowed. 'His name is Signor Khaled. But why? Do you know h—?'

She'd barely finished the words before Paolo had shrugged her from his shoulder and exploded from the seat to circle the room, pacing wildly. 'Khaled! After all this time. I knew it. I knew something was wrong.'

'What did you know? What are you talking about?'

'It's lucky I came when I did. You can't go.'

'Paolo, what on earth are you talking about?'

'Just that you mustn't go.'

'But Gianfranco's expecting me to take this commission. I can't let him down.'

'Tell him you're sick—tell him your mother's sick—tell him anything, but don't go to Jebbai.'

'This isn't making any sense. Give me one good reason why I should turn this job down. More than that, why you'd expect me to lie to get out of it.'

'Because your new client is not what he seems. I know him.'

'What? Are you implying Signor Khaled is some kind of criminal?'

'There's no "Signor Khaled" about it. Didn't he even tell you his full name?'

'His full name? I—'

He snarled. 'Your Signor Khaled is none other than Sheikh Khaled Al-Ateeq, ruler of Jebbai.'

A sheikh? Sapphy absorbed the revelation with interest, searching for the significance that Paolo obviously placed in the news. It made some sort of sense, certainly, as his whole aura spoke of power. But still she failed to see why his identity should change anything. And it was hardly a crime to protect one's title. He'd certainly made no attempt to hide his name, after all.

'So he's a sheikh? That probably explains why Gianfranco is falling all over himself to ensure I take the job. But does that change anything? What I do know is he's getting married and he's engaged me to design his bride's wedding dress. And you haven't given me one good reason why I shouldn't do it.'

'Listen to me,' Paolo said, his hands on her shoulders. 'Whatever's going on, you can't trust this man. I have no idea what he's up to, but I doubt there will even be a wedding.'

She shivered, his tone as much as his words frightening her. She tried to cover her anxiety with a laugh, but the sound came out brittle and false. 'That's ridiculous. Then why would he go to the trouble of commissioning a designer for a wedding gown?'

'To get you there.'

This time there was no covering up the tremor that rocked her. 'You're frightening me, Paolo, and I don't understand why. What makes you say these things? How do you know?'

'I just do.'

'No,' she stated, needing facts to back up this fantastic story he was building up. 'That's not good enough. If you're going to scare me with stories like this then I need some kind of proof. Why shouldn't I go? What do you have against this sheikh?'

He spun away from her, fists clenched. 'I can't tell you.' She was about to tell him that he'd have to when he wheeled back to face her. 'Except to say, he's the most ruthless man I've ever met and I know he'll stop at nothing to get what he wants.'

The client's eyes came instantly to her mind, dark and relentless as they'd all but pierced their way into her skin during their heated scrutiny. Yes, he was no doubt ruthless, but so too could Paolo be, along with half of his colleagues. You didn't make it to the top ranks of international law partnerships by being anything less.

She turned on him, protesting, 'I don't understand. If you feel this strongly about the man, why is it you've never so much as mentioned him before?'

'What happened was long ago. Before I met you.'

'Then maybe he's changed. Whatever differences you had back then probably don't exist any more.'

He shook his head. 'No. You don't know him like I do.'

'And you don't know what I do. There is a bride. I'm meeting her just as soon as we get to Jebbai.'

She knew she was stretching the truth, but with the mood Paolo was in, there was no way he wouldn't jump on the news that Khaled had prevaricated over her meeting the bride, whatever his reasons, and use it to add fuel to his arguments to stop her going.

And she wanted to go, even if it had taken her a while to convince herself. There were good business reasons for her to go. It wasn't as if Paolo would be waiting for her at home while she was gone, after all.

'Then are you so sure that she's willing to marry this man?'

'Oh, for heaven's sake. What are you suggesting? This is the twenty-first century after all. As it happens,' she added, if only to stop Paolo's wild accusations in their tracks, 'they need to get married quickly. The bride is desperately ill.' Then she added for effect, 'It's really quite romantic, don't you think?'

He watched her, saying nothing, though the fierce rise and fall of his chest spoke volumes about how he was feeling. There could have been a ten-gallon drum of romance in the situation and still it would have eluded him.

'Look,' she said softly, moving alongside and placing a hand on his rigid forearm, 'this *Sheikh Khaled*, whoever he is and whatever problems you've had with him in the past, in all likelihood has no idea that

CHAPTER THREE

HE WAS waiting for her at the airport. One glance at him through the tinted limousine windows was enough to send the courage she'd found to disregard Paolo's warnings scampering for cover. Standing next to the jet, Khaled seemed taller, even larger than he had done in the salon, his dark eyes fixed searchingly on the approaching car.

Why was she here? What if Paolo was right? What if Khaled was as dangerous as Paolo suggested? Would she have cause to regret defying him?

Already she regretted their argument. He'd left soon after, not staying for dinner, let alone for the night, and she hadn't heard from him all weekend. No doubt he'd already be winging his way back to the States.

She hated that they'd parted this way. She'd never defied him so openly or so vehemently before, but then he'd never tried to stop her from doing anything either, certainly for no valid reason. If only there'd been some sound basis to his objections, she'd have had no compunction in taking more notice.

But no, Paolo was wrong and he'd have to admit it when she returned in four weeks. Not that he was likely to be around to welcome her home, whatever his vague offer was to sort things out between them.

And even if he was, things were going to be different between them. It was just as well he hadn't stayed the night. Right now she wasn't sure what she felt for Paolo, but it sure as hell wasn't the happy-ever-after love she'd once assumed their relationship to be heading for. Things had changed between them over the past months and not for the better. A change of scenery would give her a chance to get her scrambled thoughts in order.

The driver pulled up alongside the private jet sending her thoughts into further disarray. Why on earth had she imagined they would be flying to Jebbai on a conventional airliner? Of course, she hadn't known back then that he was a sheikh. Naturally he would have his own plane, more than likely an entire fleet of them.

Then her door was opened and her insulated world in the limousine's interior was invaded by the unfettered brilliance of daylight, the roar of engines and the high-octane smell of jet fuel. In the time it took to blink he was there, at the door, offering her his hand.

'Signora Clemenger, I am so pleased you have decided to accept my commission.'

Even over the whine of engines his cultured voice flowed over her, warm and rich in a way that somehow curled into her senses.

She stepped from the car to be greeted by the wind, whipping at the loose tendrils of her hair, and his half-smile, tugging at her self-confidence. Dark eyes shone down on her, a degree of self-satisfaction plainly evident.

She bristled. He didn't have to feel smug about her compliance; it was only a job after all.

'Did you ever doubt it, *Sheikh* Khaled Al-Ateeq?'

If she hadn't been searching his face she might have missed it, that tell-tale tiny tic in his cheek, the jolt of realisation that caused his eyes to narrow fractionally.

'I see you have discovered my little secret.'

'So it would appear,' she rejoined. 'Although I very much doubt that I have discovered them all.'

He laughed, throwing his head back and taking her completely by surprise. She'd wanted to warn him, to let him know that she was no *ingénue* heading off into the desert with a stranger. Paolo's fears were way off base, she was sure, but in any event, it paid to let him know that he would have to earn her trust.

Yet he laughed in a way that sounded as if he was truly delighted. And she liked the way it sounded. Even more so, she liked the way he looked. His pale blue fine-knit sweater hugged his torso without stretching, the colour contrasting vividly against his deep olive skin, especially where the shallow V-neck revealed a tantalising slice of his chest. Fitted black trousers accentuated his firm abdomen, showing off his long legs to full effect.

There was no doubt about it; he was going to make one dashing groom. She made a mental note for her design plans—if she didn't do the right thing by the bride, Sheikh Khaled was likely to steal the show.

His head tilted back towards her, catching her frank appraisal and making her wish her eyes had found themselves a safer occupation while he laughed. But she resisted the temptation to turn them away; instead letting them stay locked on to his. He might be drop-dead handsome, but she was no teenaged schoolgirl who could be embarrassed simply by being caught out looking at a man. And he was her client after all. It wasn't as if she was interested in him for herself.

'Come,' he said at last, a smile lingering in his eyes as he ushered her towards the steps, 'we'll take care of the formalities inside.'

She took one last look around her, bidding farewell to the now familiar mountain range towering over the hangars and planes to the north of Milan's Malpensa Airport. Already her life working with Gianfranco Bacelli seemed distant as she climbed the steps into the plane, a sense of excitement building in her veins at this new adventure that not even the too-close proximity of the sheikh at her back could dispel.

He liked what she was wearing, the soft rose-coloured fabric of her dress contrasting with the blue of her eyes and her dark-gold hair, and the style was feminine without being flowery. But what he liked best was the way it moulded to her shape, showing off the roundness of her behind invitingly as she climbed the stairs.

In her wake her clean scent, a hint of perfume, light and summery, was a refreshing relief from the fume-laden air. She smelled fresh and ripe, with not a trace of the fear she'd projected when he'd offered the commission. There was something though—a wariness? Certainly her comment on greeting him had been nothing short of a challenge.

So, she suspected there was more to him than met the eye, yet still she was here. The woman had courage. So much the better. He liked nothing better than a challenge himself.

His eyes followed her progress upwards. It was a long time since he'd had a woman. Too long. He could feel the ache building even now as he watched her ascend, the natural roll of her hips accentuating the curve to her slim waist. Much, much too long.

But he could wait four weeks for this one.

She would be worth it.

And she would be his.

The *Gulfstream V* took off smoothly and ate up the miles through the air with a five-star efficiency that mirrored its internal opulence. Sapphy nestled into the soft leather upholstery of the armchair, taking a brief break from the preliminary sketches she was working on, knowing that she'd never look at air travel in quite the same way again.

The cabin had been fitted out to ensure the comfort of its passengers. The few seats were all large and luxurious, the dining setting where she was now sitting large enough for a silver-service menu, and to the rear was a business office complete with computer and fax facilities made possible by satellite-communication links. There were other rooms too, she could tell, closed off to the rear. Space, speed and luxury. Sheikh Khaled obviously travelled in style.

And so far he'd been the perfect host. He'd handled the outgoing formalities with aplomb, seen her settled and comfortable for their take-off and then he'd excused himself, retiring to the cockpit to talk to the pilot. Meanwhile the attentive stewards ensured she was supplied with everything she needed and more.

If this was a taste of how things would be in Jebbai, she had nothing at all to fear from Sheikh Khaled. Just as she'd rationalised, he would have plenty enough to keep him occupied and she'd need hardly ever see him.

The cockpit door swung open and Sapphy's eyes felt compelled to follow the movement. Khaled emerged and seemed to pause, mid-step, as his eyes met hers. Breath jagged in her chest as she saw something pass through them, something hot and hungry and real…

And then it was gone, and the corners of his mouth kicked up and he resumed his progress towards her. She turned her face back to her sketches, making random lines with her pencil, knowing the sudden burst of internal fire she was experiencing would be splashed vividly all over her face.

So much for feeling relaxed.

Then his hand was on her shoulder and her pencil jerked in her fingers as every muscle inside her clamped shut.

'Lovely,' he said, close enough to her ear as he bent down to look at her sketches that she could feel his warm breath on her cheek and there was no way he couldn't hear the pounding of her heart. She didn't dare glance sideways—he was too close, way too close.

She licked her lips, trying to focus on the sketches. 'They're just some rough ideas at this stage, but I was wondering if you have any idea which kind of style you think your bride will prefer? I don't even have a clue as to her measurements yet, so some of these may not be appropriate.'

He stayed silent for a few seconds, seconds where his hand remained on her shoulder and his breath curled against her skin. Seconds that dragged long and interminable.

'I like this one,' he said at last, pointing with his free hand to a graceful princess-line dress, scooped over the shoulders and neck and falling to a full skirt with cleverly designed pleats that revealed a complementary underskirt. 'What do you think?'

From her peripheral vision she knew he'd turned and was looking at her, waiting for her response. She breathed in, licked her lips and nodded. That particular design was her own personal favourite from the half-dozen scattered over the table. It was elegant, stunning in its simplicity, and yet regal enough for a princess.

'If you think it will suit her,' she offered, turning her head fractionally towards him at last, while still directing her eyes anywhere but on his face.

'Oh, yes,' he said, his voice low and husky. 'I think it will be perfect…'

She lifted her eyes to his and her mouth went dry. 'Just perfect.'

He was close. Too close. So close she could taste his breath on hers. So close she could see herself reflected in the dark mirror of his eyes. So close she had cause to wonder whether Paolo's warnings hadn't been somewhere near the mark. This was no ordinary man. Had she done the wrong thing by coming after all?

Yet why did she seem to freeze when she should be doing something—anything? And he wasn't pulling away. If she wasn't mistaken, he was getting even closer...

This wasn't happening! She jerked her head away and leaned forward, scrabbling with the papers on the table in a poor interpretation of organising them. 'That's great,' she said. 'I'll keep working on that design if it suits you. And as soon as I have some measurements, I'll make some real progress.'

She knew she was babbling but it kept her mouth busy and right now that seemed the most important thing on earth. The way he'd looked at her lips. Surely he hadn't been going to kiss her? He was a man about to get married after all.

She must have been imagining it. Paolo's words had poisoned her. Was it possible to suffer altitude sickness in a pressurised aircraft?

She was aware of him standing upright and his hand left her shoulder at last. Strange, it had been there so long, it almost felt cold now that he'd removed it.

'This calls for champagne,' he said, gesturing to the stewards. He sat down in the chair alongside her as if nothing had just happened as a steward delivered two champagne flutes and an ice bucket containing a chilled bottle of sparkling wine. She recognised the label instantly.

'Australian wine?'

He dipped his head a fraction. 'In your honour. I thought you might like a taste of your homeland, seeing as I was taking you away even from your adopted city.'

A swell of warmth moved through her as she was strangely touched by the gesture. She'd expected, from the luxury of the plane, that for him it would be *Dom Perignon* or nothing. To choose an Australian wine, a simply stunning Australian wine none the less, was something she'd never expected. And he'd done it to make her feel at home?

How did he do this to her? How could he make her feel so on edge one minute, so considered the next?

The sparkling wine was poured and he handed her a flute. 'I propose a toast,' he said. 'To a gown that is going to be as breathtaking as the astonishing woman who designs it.'

He raised his glass to her, his eyes half shuttered, smiling at her purposefully before lifting the glass to his lips. His eyes never left her, even as his chin kicked up, his eyes stayed with her, dark, intent.

She swallowed before even taking as much as a sip as her feelings of comfort rocked into uncertainty again. Maybe it was time to remind him of another woman who would play a part in this wedding, a woman who, it now occurred to her, he barely spoke about.

'Thank you,' she said softly. 'And if I may, I'd like to propose a toast to the woman who will wear the dress, for without her, the dress is nothing. To your bride.'

She took a sip from her crystal flute, satisfied that she'd put their relationship back into some kind of perspective. Whether or not he'd intended to kiss her just then, he'd at least know that she wasn't likely to forget he was about to marry another woman.

But, watching him over the rim of her glass, she could see her words didn't faze him in the least. If anything, they just served to increase the width of his smile, the dark intent in his eyes.

'Absolutely,' he said. 'Let us drink to the woman who will be my wife. To my bride.'

He raised his flute and held it up to her again, still smiling, holding her gaze firm and square, and just for one moment she sensed she was missing something.

Something had happened—oh, yes, he'd acknowledged his bride and he'd done it without missing a beat. But there was something else, curious and intriguing, that she couldn't quite pin down. Something that didn't feel quite right.

Her glass moved to her lips mechanically and she had her first taste of the sparkling wine, the tiny bead bursting with the essence of yeast and fruit and neither too sweet nor too dry. But her appreciation of

the wine came a poor second to the continued mach-
inations of her mind. Just what was Sheikh Khaled
about? She didn't want to give credence to Paolo's
concerns but there was something about him that dis-
turbed her on the deepest level.

And yet she'd never been in the company of roy-
alty before. Was it any wonder he was complex and
guarded? It was probably bred into him, along with
his power. Was it any wonder he was different from
other men?

Paolo's words were rendering her too suspicious,
too sensitive to the merest inflexion of Khaled's voice
and too ready to think the worst.

Sheikh Khaled was clearly a gracious host. She
should relax and enjoy the experience. That way she
would prove Paolo's fears groundless.

A steward leaned over and whispered something in
Khaled's ear, his eyes widening a fraction before they
narrowed on a razor-sharp gleam.

'I apologise,' he said, putting down his glass.
'Something has arisen which I must attend to urgently. Please excuse me.'

She looked over to the business workstation, where
two uniformed officers were already gathered around
the computer screen. 'Is anything the matter?' she
asked.

'It is a trifling matter, nothing to concern yourself
with,' he assured her, nodding before turning and
withdrawing to join his staff. Where had his officers
come from? She hadn't noticed them on the plane

earlier, although it no doubt made sense for someone of a sheikh's standing to travel with his own security.

Whatever the 'trifling matter' was, it was taking some time. And emotion. Every now and then the sound of raised voices and urgent instructions drowned out the constant hum of the engines and the sudden noise would pull her out of her designs once more to wonder what was going on. But the men were engaged in rapid-fire discussions between themselves and someone at the end of the satellite phone line and there was no way her curiosity would outweigh her good sense. She was staying right here.

Besides, it was a welcome break to have time away from Khaled's presence, his dark, challenging eyes and his unreadable expressions.

A slight change in the feel of the flight told her they'd started their descent. She looked out of the window to the ground some forty thousand feet below. They were crossing a coastline, the blue waters of what she took to be the Mediterranean a stark contrast to the white line of the coast and the wide expanse of yellow-brown interior beyond.

She turned back to find Khaled lowering himself into the seat next to her.

'It won't be long now,' he said.

'Is everything all right?' she asked, with a glance to the rear of the plane, but the two officers had disappeared again.

'It is now,' he said, noncommittally.

It wasn't long before the sleek aircraft gently touched down on the runway at Jebbai's airport, a short distance, Khaled explained, from the capital, Hebra. Sapphy stepped from the plane into the clean, dry heat of a Jebbai afternoon. She paused for a moment at the top of the steps. It was so different from Milan—with no mountains to shadow the small but modern airport. Instead the land was flat, reaching in all directions around, one endless golden dune after another, leading on to the horizon and broken only by a long strip of bitumen, the highway leading to the capital.

The middle of nowhere.

Never had the phrase been so apt. She gulped down a fortifying lungful of air.

Never had she felt so alone.

Khaled's hand squeezed her shoulder, as if reassuring her. 'Welcome to your new home,' he said. She was halfway down the stairs and the moment gone before she realised what he'd said.

They transferred to the waiting limousine for the thirty-minute drive as day was beginning to fade. The heat of the day lingered, the warm air clean and dry under a sky that seemed to go on forever.

They said little for the first few minutes, Sapphy content to gaze out of the windows and drink in the view, finding even the passing dunes and rock formations fascinating, barely able to contain her excitement at the harsh beauty of the landscape. Even the presence of Khaled by her side wasn't enough to quell her enthusiasm. Already she was brimming with ideas about colour, patterns and texture. The landscape was like a breath of fresh air.

'What do you think of my country?'

'It's beautiful, just beautiful.'

'Never take the desert for granted. It's harsh and dangerous and unforgiving.'

She looked over to him, surprised by his words. 'Of course, but isn't the danger what gives it the edge over, say, a landscape of green hills and valleys? There the land is lush and fertile, beautiful in its own way, yet soft and safe. Whereas this place has colour and drama and magnificence that goes hand in hand with danger. Even more,' she licked her lips, searching the view outside her window for the right words, 'there's almost a timeless quality about it. Almost like it's waiting for something...'

She turned back to him, still struggling for the right way to finish her sentence, only to have the breath snag in her throat as a shudder rippled through her.

His eyes trapped her, ensnaring her in a blistering gaze that burned and sizzled her to the core. Whatever she had been going to say was incinerated in raw heat.

His heat.

He moved closer, reaching out a hand to cup her jaw. She flinched at his touch but his fingers held her firm, scorching the skin of her neck and chin. 'Your eyes blaze when you talk of such things. They reflect the light like the facets of a well-cut stone. How appropriately they named you.'

She swallowed, a vain attempt to lubricate her ashen throat.

'Such beautiful eyes. Tell me, is their beauty like your green landscape, lush and fertile, or is it a dangerous magnificence that shines within them? Which is it, I wonder?'

She shook her head, the little she was able, her tongue attempting to moisten her lips. 'I don't know.' She raised a hand to his forearm. 'I've never thought about it.' *Maybe she could brush him away...* Then her hand met his arm, the sheer strength of his limb clearly evident through the fine-knit fabric. His arm was like steel, sculptured tensile steel.

There was no brushing this man away.

His head tilted to one side, his lips turned up into a lazy grin, as if amused by her attempts to rescue herself from his grasp. His grip relaxed.

'Yet your prose suggests you are very perceptive. You see qualities in the desert that others miss. I find it difficult to believe you would not have the same talent when applied to people.'

No question which type you fall into, she thought in a rush. *Tall, dark and dangerous.* 'I really don't see how this is relevant,' she murmured on a breath, closing her eyes for a second and wondering if he could have heard her over the hammering in her veins. 'And I'd prefer it if you didn't touch me.'

He raised his eyebrows in a way that suggested he didn't believe her, but still he shrugged and relaxed his grip on her jaw.

'As you wish,' he said.

Her chin kicked up in relief, but it was to be short-lived as his large hand didn't pull completely away but continued to sweep slowly down the line of her throat, searing a trail of scorching sensation. His fingers spanned the open neck of her dress, skimming lightly under the cross-over neckline before his hand finally withdrew.

She sucked in a breath as naked sensation skittered through her, a charge so electric that her breasts tingled and firmed.

She didn't want him to touch her, didn't want him anywhere near her, so why did her senses continue to hum, her breasts continue to swell, when his hand was long gone? The view out of the window stared blankly back at her, offering no answers, but there was no way she'd risk looking anywhere but outside the car, at least not until her breathing and pulse were back under control. Once they were in the palace she would have to stay right away from Sheikh Khaled. He was far too unpredictable, far too compelling.

Far too dangerous.

Yet a good measure of that danger came from within herself. There was no way she could deny she was attracted to him. His physical presence was enough to rock her to her foundations.

His touch was something else.

She'd just have to stay right out of his reach.

Something ahead caught her interest. There were buildings appearing in the twilight, low flat dwellings at first and then higher-rise, with balconies and the muted shadows of palm trees swaying against their walls. Domes of mosques and minarets interrupted the otherwise predominantly horizontal skyline until the approaching city-centre skyscrapers changed the aspect to vertical. And there were people, gathered along the road, the lights from cigarettes like tiny fireflies spinning in the gathering darkness.

She was just about to turn and ask Khaled if they were in Hebra when their world exploded.

CHAPTER FOUR

THE car rocked with the noise and the force of the explosion as dazzling red and white light turned the interior of the car into a crazy frozen snapshot. She shrieked and jumped across the divide between them, throwing herself into Khaled's arms and burying her head in his chest as a barrage of noise rained down on them.

His heartbeat sounded calm and steady in her ear; already she felt safer with his arms wrapped tightly around her, protecting her, keeping her safe.

More colours lit the sky, green, blue, as cheers from the onlookers filled the spaces between the blasts. Children squealed, not in terror, but in delight.

Fireworks, she realised the instant after she'd plastered herself to his chest; she was getting scared witless over a few fireworks.

And look where it had got her! She was practically sitting in his lap.

She wrenched back her head, away from the comforting rhythm of his heart, the rock-steady safety of his chest, trying to peel herself away without further touching him. If only he'd relax his arms!

'You make it difficult for me not to touch you,' he said with a kernel of humour that had been noticeably absent in his voice until now, 'if you insist on throwing yourself at me like that.'

'I thought... I mean...' It would sound so stupid that she couldn't bring herself to say the words. She pushed back against the circle of his arms, still painfully aware that fabric didn't count for much when your thighs were pressed this close to his. 'Please, you can let me go now.'

'And have you get frightened again? Maybe you should relax,' he suggested. 'Enjoy the fireworks.'

She looked up at him, the strong planes of his face thrown into sharp relief by the crazy colours exploding in the sky. 'What's going on?'

'My people are welcoming back their sheikh.'

'You're kidding. They do this every time you come back?'

He laughed, rich and soft, a sound that reminded her of the smoothest coffee and cream. 'My people are very excited about the wedding and their new queen. This is the start of a month-long celebration in Jebbai.'

'Then I suggest,' she said, levering herself further away from him, 'that it's not such a great idea for your people to see you like this with your bride's dress designer.'

'I wouldn't worry too much,' he said, releasing her all the same so she could scramble back to the opposite side of the wide leather seat. 'My people are under no misapprehension as to who you are.'

She looked at him sharply. He was speaking in riddles again and she didn't want to play his game. She stayed silent as they continued through the city, amazed at the contrast of the old and the new; the ancient-looking mosques, timeless and elegant, the piercing skyscrapers, modern architectural master-pieces—Hebra had it all.

Eventually the car slowed to a crawl outside a pair of massive timber and iron gates swinging slowly open, which thudded resoundingly shut behind them as the car pulled into a large courtyard. A small wel-coming party stood waiting.

He took her hand and squeezed it gently. 'Welcome to my home,' he said before the doors both sides were pulled open and he dropped her hand to alight.

She stepped out onto the ancient cobbled courtyard before the tall palace that was to be her home for the next four weeks. It was magnificent even in the dark of night with spotlights strategically placed to illu-minate the walls and the towers. In the light of day it would be spectacular, its creamy walls studded with mother-of-pearl and tortoiseshell, giving a sumptuous appearance and texture.

Khaled's hand pressed against the small of her back, and she let him guide her to meet the small group waiting for them. A tall man in traditional dress, his face lean and hollow, his beard greying and neatly trimmed and his eyes bearing a strong resem-blance to Khaled's, stepped down to greet them.

'Saleem,' said Khaled, embracing the man, 'let me introduce you to the famous designer, Sapphire Clemenger, from the House of Bacelli in Milan. Sapphy, this is my cousin, Saleem.'

Saleem took her hand, bowing over it graciously before he raised his head and looked up at her, the sudden glint in his eyes sending ice-cold spiders crawling down her spine. 'Welcome to Jebbai,' he said, his mouth curved into what she supposed was intended to pass as a smile.

She'd never experienced anything less welcoming, but managed somehow to crack the layer of ice he'd submerged her under enough to dredge up a smile of her own and murmur her thanks before the rest of the party was briefly introduced. Finally a shy-looking young woman was presented to her.

'This is Azizah,' Khaled told her as the girl bowed. 'She will be your maid.'

She smiled again, much more genuinely this time, and took the girl's hand. 'So you are to help me with the dressmaking?'

'No,' interrupted Khaled, before the girl could respond. 'You will have a staff of ten to help you construct the dress. They will be here first thing in the morning for your instruction. Azizah is your personal maid. She will do whatever you ask.'

'That's hardly necessary,' she protested. 'I won't need an entire staff to make one dress.'

'You have only four weeks and you were the one who thought that was not enough time—remember? So, you have staff. Now, let me show you to your accommodation.' His hand at her back, he urged her up the wide steps to the large keyhole-style opening leading inside.

'Surely the girl can show her to her quarters,'

Saleem's heavily accented English broke in. 'There are matters of state to discuss.'

Khaled wheeled and turned on his cousin. 'Five minutes will make no difference. I will show Miss Clemenger to her quarters. *Then* I will meet you in the library.'

She shuddered as he directed her inside the palace. 'Are you cold?' he asked, surprising her by even noticing.

'No.' The palace interior's temperature was even and comfortable, the air sweet with the faint hint of incense. No doubt thick walls would keep the interior bearable on even the hottest day.

'Then what's wrong?

'Tell me,' he insisted, when still she hadn't answered. 'You're my responsibility now.'

'It's probably nothing—it's just your cousin, Saleem; I get the impression he doesn't like me.'

'He will have to get used to you.'

'Do you think so? In just four weeks?' Khaled glared sharply down at her as he led her through a wide marble pillared reception hall.

'Well, if he doesn't like me now, I'm not sure what I can do to change things in barely a month.'

'It will pay you not to upset Saleem. He is family. Things are different here to how they are done in Milan or even in Australia.'

Sapphy opened her mouth to protest that Saleem already seemed upset enough with her without her doing a thing, but then snapped it shut before uttering a word. What was the point? He was right. Things were bound to be different here. It would just be easier if she didn't feel such an intruder—Saleem had made it crystal clear that he didn't welcome her presence.

But it was only for four weeks after all, maybe less if she could complete the dress early. So the sooner she got stuck into making the wedding dress, the sooner she could return to Milan.

After walking along passageway after passageway, Khaled finally showed her into a reception-cum-sitting room, large and spacious. 'This is your study,' he said, waving his arm over the luxurious lounge suite and the substantial desk, complete with paper and writing tools. 'And this,' he said showing her through into an adjoining room, 'is your workshop. I trust you have everything you need. If not, just ask.'

Sapphy's eyes opened in wonder as she followed him. The room was enormous, at least twice the size of her apartment in Milan and then some. Worktables were arranged at intervals, many topped with sewing machines, all serious industrial models, she noticed as she wandered between them, not simple home dressmaking machines. Bolts of fabric lined the walls—silk, satin, brocade and laces in every bridal colour and tone imaginable. Tubs of beads and sequins, pearls and buttons were stacked on a bench. She'd seen fabric shops with less stock.

'It's incredible. How did you know?' she asked, her eyes still wide with wonder as she attempted to take it all in.

'Gianfranco told me what you might need. It was then a simple matter to have it delivered.'

'No,' she said, turning her eyes up to his. 'How did you know I would come? You couldn't be sure I would agree until today.'

Something fused, deep in his eyes, as he eliminated the distance between them with three quick-fire steps. All at once she was craning her neck up to where he stood before her. A muscle worked in his jaw as he reached out a hand. For a moment she flinched, not wanting him to grab hold of her as he'd done earlier in the car, but this time his touch was feather-light as he traced a slow line from her forehead to her jaw with just the pads of his long fingers.

'*I* was sure. I knew you would come.'

His voice was low with a husky new quality that sent tremors through her, compounding the sensations he'd stirred in her skin. She sucked in a breath that was too light on oxygen, too heavy on raw male sexuality. The pad of his thumb brushed over her lips and she tasted him, his salty heat further stirring her senses into disarray.

Her mind was a mess. Thoughts came and collided with no hint of logic or resolution. How could he have known she would come to Jebbai when she hadn't even known herself? How could he have been so certain?

And why did just one look from his dark eyes make her feel so liquid?

His fingers tilted her chin, so there was no way she could avoid his searing gaze, no way she couldn't notice his wide lips, slightly parted, no way she couldn't imagine what they would feel like on hers.

Anticipate them on hers.

'What I didn't know,' he said, his breath curling around her in the space between them, warm and hypnotic, 'was just how perfect you would be.'

She read his last words on her lips as his mouth descended over hers, warm and gentling, and the contrast in the man struck her. He appeared so strong and hard, upright and defiant, he looked every part the ruler of his kingdom, and yet his kiss was so tender, so sweet, it seemed to squeeze something from her even as it rocked her to her soul. The power was there, lurking just below the surface, but there was so much more besides, so many nuances, so many textures to experience—the softness of his lips, the nip of his teeth, the rasp of his shadowed chin...

She felt her internal thermostat reset itself to slow burn as his mouth gently plundered her own, exploring, manipulating.

She felt his hands at her shoulders, behind her neck, down her back, their gathering touch strangely compelling. They invited her closer and she complied, leaning into the kiss and feeling the press of his firm chest against her own tight breasts.

Then he was gone from her and she blinked, swaying and throwing out a hand to the neighbouring table to steady herself, embarrassed and ashamed as she realised just how easily she'd let herself be manipulated into that kiss. Hardly the mark of a professional on her first day on the job.

'That was a mistake,' she whispered, her voice unusually thick, her hand covering lips still excruciatingly sensitised.

'We had to stop,' he said, one side of his mouth kicked up in a lazy grin. 'Saleem is waiting for me.'

'No!' She spun around, hugging her arms to herself. 'It was a mistake to kiss me. You're getting married. I have a b… I have a boyfriend. It's wrong.'

'You appeared to have no trouble forgetting your so-called "boyfriend" just then. Or do you just make a habit of forgetting him whenever it suits you?'

'Of course not!' she insisted. She had never been unfaithful to Paolo, never even thought about another man until now, when their relationship seemed stalled and their differences all the while harder to broach.

Though that wasn't the entire truth. She'd never considered any other man until Khaled had stormed onto the scene and into her life, all rampant testosterone and masculine force. 'Although you make a veritable art form of regularly forgetting you will soon have a wife.'

He came up quickly behind her and by the time she'd turned in surprise he had one arm planted firmly either side of her, trapping her against the long workbench. 'I don't forget,' he said, leaning into her, his voice tight and betraying a rising sense of fury. 'If you must know, I'm very much looking forward to it.'

He dropped his arms and wheeled away, leaving her breathless and dizzy, her mind scrambling to make sense of his words.

'I must meet with Saleem. Afterwards we will dine together—Azizah will show you the way. Meanwhile there is one more room,' he said, thrusting out an arm to indicate a door opposite. 'Do you wish me to show it to you?'

'What's in there?'

'Your bedroom.'

She swallowed, feeling solid colour infuse her cheeks. 'No, thank you. I'll manage.'

She could still recall the amused look on his face at her prim response, long after he was gone.

Dinner was a subdued affair. Saleem ignored her for the most part, directing most of his conversation at Khaled, which suited her just fine. Not that she was interested in chatting too much to Khaled either. While there were questions she wanted to ask, about his family and the history of Jebbai, she was still too shaken by the episode in the workroom. The last thing she needed to do was show him any encouragement.

It was easier to look more interested in the food. The array of spiced meats, salads and dips was laid out invitingly on the low table between them as they reclined on colourful silk cushions. She tried to focus on the spread, to sample the different tastes, all the while biding her time until she thought it was safe to excuse herself and withdraw to bed.

But her thoughts were elsewhere. She'd flung her relationship with Paolo in Khaled's face, a convenient defence in fending off his unwelcome advances, but she'd stumbled over the word 'boyfriend' as if it had been an effort. Why didn't that bother her more when it hinted that the problems they'd dredged up during their argument were more deep-seated than she'd thought? Why was it so hard to even think of Paolo as her boyfriend now?

They would talk some time after her return, he'd promised. She should hold that thought. Instead, on some deeper, instinctive level, she suspected their relationship was already beyond salvage.

Her thoughts in turmoil with the stresses of the last few days, she allowed herself one tiny cup of thick, sweet coffee before she sensed her opportunity to excuse herself. She stood, hoping to make a smooth getaway.

'Sapphire, you're not leaving us already?'

'I'm sorry, Khaled,' she replied, trying to ignore the long, hard glare she earned from Saleem, 'it's been a long day and I wish to get started early in the morning.'

'Of course,' he said, 'I should have realised. Is there anything else that you need?'

'Only some idea when I might get to meet your bride. It would be good to at least talk to her about the design before I get too far along the process.'

Saleem uttered something rapid-fire and urgent in Arabic. Khaled answered simply and briefly in English, 'No,' at which response Saleem's nostrils flared and he rose from the cushions, muttering a few more words in his cousin's direction as he stormed out without another glance at her.

'Did I say something wrong?' she asked, recalling Khaled's warning not to upset his cousin.

He shrugged. 'Saleem is…anxious, as are we all, for the welfare of the bride. Now is not a good time. I will let you know when she is available.'

'Is she in the palace?'

'Oh, yes,' he said, his eyes sparkling. 'She is already here, but she is not yet ready for the excitement of the wedding. It is too early. I will tell you when.'

'But it will be soon?'

He nodded. 'Indeed, it will be soon.'

It would have to do. She bade him goodnight and turned to go. Work on the dress would have to commence as best it could. And some time soon she'd have to hope for a series of fittings, while there was still time to make any adjustments if necessary.

'Oh, and one more thing.'

'Yes?' she said, looking over her shoulder.

'Everyone who is a guest of the palace receives a gift.'

'That's not necessary,' she said, shaking her head. 'I'm working here—'

He held up his hand in a stop gesture. 'It is necessary. You are still my guest. And you will receive traditional Jebbai garments as your gift. You would not think of offending Hebra's finest dressmakers surely? They are most honoured to be designing something for you, a famous designer from the fashion capital of Milan.'

'No,' she conceded. 'Of course I wouldn't want to offend them. Thank you.'

'Good,' he said with an air of finality. 'Someone will be sent to measure you for them tomorrow morning. Goodnight.'

CHAPTER FIVE

SAPPHY threw herself into her work over the next few days. She organised her staff, planning a schedule and putting those she could to work immediately. She'd never had so many people to work on her designs so in one way it was luxury, in another it was a challenge keeping them all occupied and coordinating what they were doing.

But they were excellent. It was clear straight away that Khaled had supplied her with top dressmakers and seamstresses, expert at sewing and beading. Some she'd been able to set tasks immediately, to work on the delicate veil, or bead the intricate panels that would be inset later into the dress. Even the language difficulties she'd expected didn't eventuate.

And while she hadn't been permitted to meet with the bride, she'd been provided with a set of measurements, allowing her to draft the pattern and run up a model in a simple fabric to test the design. And now, one short week after her arrival in Jebbai, the dress itself was starting to take shape.

Her new life was taking shape too, already assuming some kind of pattern. In the mornings she took breakfast in her suite, usually fresh fruit with dates, dried figs and creamy yoghurt, while she arranged her schedule for the day.

Then she would work solidly until four or five o'clock, depending on the day's progress. While her staff took a midday break she inspected their work, which was for the most part faultless, and that ensured better than anticipated progress.

Azizah would let her know when it was time for the evening meal and, as she had on the first evening, she would join in a shared meal with Khaled and Saleem. Khaled would ask after her health and seek a report on the dress, and she would tell him what he wished to know.

She was still reluctant to open up and talk freely with Saleem present—somehow she didn't feel comfortable with him knowing anything about her and it was clear he didn't welcome her input. So for the most part she left the two men to discuss matters amongst themselves and she'd then excuse herself after coffee, removing herself while doing her best to ignore Saleem's frosty glare and Khaled's hooded gaze.

It wasn't exactly pleasant, but at least now she was becoming used to the routine and learning not to feel so uptight in their presence.

Tonight something was different though. She looked around the dining room at the appointed time but no cold stares returned her own. Khaled sat alone amidst the plump cushions.

'Come,' he said, beckoning her to join him.

'Saleem?' she asked, lowering herself opposite.

'Is away.' He poured her a glass of tea. 'I'm afraid you're going to be stuck with just me for tonight.' He handed her the small glass and held on, even when she'd moved to take it from him.

Her eyes found his and caught the crinkle at the sides.

He was laughing at her.

'Lucky me,' she said, wresting the glass from his grasp, suddenly ruing Saleem's absence. His resentful disposition seemed suddenly preferable to Khaled's unwelcome jibes. 'Tell me,' she said, looking to wipe the smug look from his face and regain the initiative, 'how is your fiancée?'

With coffee came Sapphy's chance to make her usual quick exit.

'Are you in a hurry to leave?' he asked.

'Not at all,' she lied, when all she wanted to do was escape. Dinner had been tense after their early jibes and more than once she'd caught his brooding eyes fixed on her, surveying her. But why?

'Then come,' he said, rising from the cushions and holding out his hand. 'I want to show you something.'

'Where are you taking me?' she asked, as he led her into a part of the palace she'd never been before. He'd taken her through a seeming labyrinth of passageways, up and down short stairways and turning this way and that, so much so that she wasn't sure she'd ever be able to find her way back by herself.

'You'll see,' he said, finally leading her through a large, richly decorated doorway. She followed him through and stepped into another world.

Lush greenery surrounded her, softly lit with

torches flickering shadows against the ferns, palms and vines. Scented flowers perfumed the air, sweet and rich. They were in a large courtyard, completely enclosed by the palace, but the foliage was so tall in places that you could imagine you were miles from civilisation. From somewhere unseen came the splash of water, setting a musical backdrop, while the exotic call of birds settling down for the evening provided an accompaniment.

'It's the most beautiful garden I've ever seen,' she said as she wandered along the marble-paved walkways lined with clipped shrubs and stone. She recognised a few of the plants and bushes—myrtle, bay trees, even a grove of orange trees, their coloured fruit standing out against the foliage as brightly as ornaments on a Christmas tree.

He reached up alongside her and plucked one of the oranges from the tree and handed the heavy fruit to her solemnly.

'The best oranges either side of the Tigris,' he said before he twisted off another for himself, studying it, weighing it in his hands as he talked.

'This was my mother's favourite place. My father had it planted for her as a wedding present.'

She looked up at him. It was the first time he'd ever referred to his parents. Apart from Saleem, she knew nothing at all of his family. She touched his forearm gently.

'Tell me about them.'

Even in the muted light, she saw the darkness swirl in his eyes, felt the tension in his corded arm, and for a moment she thought he wasn't going to respond. Then he uttered a deep sigh and turned down the path, taking her with him.

'My mother was a Frenchwoman, a model turned successful actress. And very, very beautiful. My father saw her on the screen and fell in love with her at first sight. He went to Paris and wooed her and brought her back to be his wife.'

A French mother. An Arab father. And no doubt a university education in Europe somewhere. His blend of accents suddenly made sense. No wonder he'd been so difficult to place.

'What happened to your mother's film career? Did she continue making movies?'

'Not once she married my father.'

'She gave it all up? She left everything behind, her career, her stardom, to come here and be someone's wife?'

'Does that surprise you? My father was a very good-looking man. He was also very persuasive and he wanted her.'

'But what about what she wanted? Times might have been different then, but didn't she get some say in it?'

'She wasn't a prisoner here. She could have left any time. But she fell in love with my father and they were married. They were very happy together. Very happy.'

She matched his steps along the marble flagstones, marvelling at the constantly changing views at each turn, feeling the magic of the garden permeate her soul. It was so peaceful here, so beautiful. Was it enough, though, to make someone abandon their former life?

'She must have loved him very much,' she said at last and he nodded silently, seemingly lost in his own thoughts.

Yet for all the apparent romance, there was clearly no happy ending to this story. She could sense it in his mounting tension, she could sense it in the air that fairly crackled around him.

'What happened to them?'

He brought her to a halt alongside a large tiered fountain, staring without focus at the marble animals, the deer and antelope, the birds and the fish, playfully squirting streams of water from their mouths. It was a work of art but she could tell he saw nothing of the artisans' skill, nothing of the beauty of the piece as his mind fixed on another event, another time. 'They were killed by an avalanche,' he said, his voice strangely flat. 'They were supposed to be in London but there was a sudden change of plan.' He paused. 'They ended up going to the Alps instead…'

His words trailed off, lost in the burble of the fountain.

'That's terrible,' she said. 'I'm so sorry.' She knew it was painfully inadequate but there was nothing more she could offer.

'They should have been in London,' he asserted, the volume in his voice rising. 'If they'd been in London, they would never have been swept away. They would never have been killed.'

His vehemence tipped her off. For whatever reason Khaled obviously held himself responsible for his parents' change of plan. 'You mustn't blame yourself,' she offered.

His eyes blasted cold fury down onto her, his face all brutal angles and harsh planes in the soft light from the torches.

'That's where you're wrong,' he muttered through clenched teeth. 'It's not me that I blame.'

He turned and stormed off, leaving the sharp tang of orange peel piercing the turbulent air in his wake. A flash of colour on the ground caught her eye. It was his orange. She picked it up, assuming he'd dropped it in his rush to get away.

Until she saw the imprints left by his fingers, the angry wounds caused by his nails, puncturing the skin and pulverising the flesh with such force that, compared to hers, the inside of his orange was no more than pulp.

It had been a mistake to take her there. Instead of making her feel more at ease with him, all he'd done was dredge up the hate from deep inside him until it spilled over, fetid and rank.

But he would have his revenge. It was now so close he could taste it. And it would be sweeter than he'd ever imagined.

The dress was nearing completion. It was going to be magnificent, without a doubt the most beautiful wedding dress she'd designed. Even the champagne-coloured silk dress she'd whipped up for her own sister, Opal's, wedding in Sydney two years ago and that she'd been so proud of couldn't hold a candle to this design.

All it now needed was a fitting or two and the seams could be completed, the length tweaked and the finishing touches made. And all Khaled had to do was agree to her request to allow her just one hour with the bride, instead of continually frustrating her with excuses and deferments.

He'd hardly spoken to her since that strange night a week ago in the gardens when his barely restrained fury had been a palpable thing and his cryptic words still haunted her. For some reason she'd upped the ante on his emotions that night in a way that made her feel that somehow, in some strange and inexplicable way, *she* was responsible for the death of his parents.

But that was crazy. She'd grown up on the other side of the world. She'd never had anything to do with the royal family of Jebbai. It didn't make sense.

She tried to push these thoughts aside as she sat at her desk, writing postcards in the hour before lunch. She'd sent her staff home early as, until Khaled agreed to a fitting, there was nothing more for them to do. She'd already completed brief greetings for her family, her mother and sisters back in Australia. It was the last postcard she wavered over.

What should she say to Paolo?

Her mobile phone was useless out here and in a way she was glad. She wanted Paolo to contact her first. But he hadn't made any attempt. They hadn't spoken since their argument in Milan and somehow 'the weather's fine, wish you were here' didn't cut it. So why couldn't she think of anything to write?

Part of her wanted to reach out and repair the damage to their relationship. The other part of her was still angry with him. He'd scared her half mad with his predictions of disaster in Jebbai, done his best to put her off going. And without offering a shred of evidence to support his crazy claims.

Without a doubt Khaled was a force to be reckoned with. Certainly he had issues with the tragic death of his parents, but was that so unusual?

Whatever, surely it should be easier to recall exactly how Paolo looked while she attempted to write this postcard? Instead her thoughts were infused with the shadow of a tall, dark-eyed man, brooding and magnetic, emphatic and compulsive. Why did he come to mind so easily when pictures of Paolo were proving so difficult to summon? Why was it so hard to forget about him?

A knock on the door interrupted her thoughts. 'Come in,' she called without looking up, expecting Azizah to be returning from some errand or advising her that the midday meal was ready.

'Am I interrupting you?'

Her head snapped up to where he stood inside the door, looking down at her. She shivered. He hadn't been in her rooms since the day she'd arrived. Somehow the large room seemed shrunken with him in it. He strode closer to the desk, pouncing on the postcard she was toying with. She hadn't managed to get further than the address and 'Dear Paolo'. A nerve in his cheek twitched. Her heart jumped wildly in her chest. They'd never discussed Paolo by name so how would Khaled react to seeing her postcard addressed to him? And would he recall their differences as clearly and as vehemently as had Paolo?

'Missing your boyfriend?'

Her blood formed an icy crust. 'Who said he was my boyfriend?'

His eyebrows lifted. 'Fair question,' he said. 'Maybe "lover" would be more appropriate.'

Her knuckles tightened as she screwed her fingers tighter around her pen. 'I haven't finished that.'

'On the contrary, you haven't started it. Nothing to say after so long apart?'

She kicked up her chin. She wasn't going to discuss Paolo and their relationship with anybody, least of all with Khaled. 'The dress is just about complete,' she said, switching topics. 'When are you going to agree to my request for a fitting with the bride?'

He flicked the card back down onto the desk. 'She knows what you're doing. There's no rush.'

'On the contrary,' she said, reiterating his own words for emphasis, 'there's every reason to rush. You have two weeks until this wedding and if I can complete this gown now, that's one major thing out of the way and then I can go home. I need just one fitting with the bride and my work is almost done.'

He lunged towards the desk and spread his arms down wide around her, his face dipping closer to hers.

'Are you in such a hurry to return to your lover? Why so, when he has made no attempt to contact you in all the time you have been here?'

'How do you know he hasn't?'

'Has he?' he challenged.

She refused to let her gaze fall. She would not be drawn into whatever game Khaled was playing.

'The dress is almost ready,' she repeated. 'When do I get my fitting?'

'Show me,' he said.

She was grateful for the opportunity to get up from her desk and burn up some of her nervous tension, if only by walking to the next room. She led the way into the workroom, where the almost completed garment sat on the model set up according to the measurements provided. Even on something as inanimate as a headless arrangement of metal and padding the dress was sensational. She felt a surge of pride just looking at it. Together with the team that Khaled had assembled for her, she'd turned a rough sketch into a dress that would turn its wearer into a princess. It would be perfect.

Or it could be, if only she could be guaranteed a fitting before the big day.

'Here it is,' she said. 'Now, when do I get my fitting?'

'When I say so.'

'*I* am the designer here and I say that I need to have a fitting now.'

'The bride is not ready.'

'This is crazy. If your bride cannot manage to turn

up for a fitting, how can you be so sure she'll turn up for the wedding?'

'She'll be there.'

'You think so?' She hesitated, almost afraid to put to voice the thoughts her mind was now throwing around. 'You know, I thought she must be desperately sick, that's why the secrecy, that's why her non-appearance for a fitting and her complete non-involvement in this wedding. Yet you don't act like the husband-to-be of an ill woman. Something's not right. She's not sick, is she?'

'I never said she was ill.'

'You let me believe she was.' It was an accusation.

He shrugged. 'What you choose to believe is up to you.'

'But then, why else would she be so invisible? What other reason can there be for her not wanting to be involved in her own wedding?'

Her mind churned, wheels turning as the fight she'd had with Paolo came into sharp relief. He'd warned her that things weren't right. The shudder that moved through her chilled her to the bone. She gritted her teeth to prevent them chattering as the knowledge of what he was doing seeped into her consciousness.

'I have to question whether there even is a bride,' she whispered, when at last the tremors in her body had stilled enough for her to talk. 'That would explain why she's not exactly champing at the bit to walk down the aisle with you. I've been here for two weeks without catching a glimpse of her. Nobody talks about her and I don't even think she's got a name. You've certainly never mentioned it. There's no bride and no wedding and no reason for me to be here. Yet I don't understand—'

'There is a bride!'

'Oh? Then maybe Paolo was right. I should have listened to him. He warned me this was on the cards, that even if there was a bride, she might be less than willing.

'Is that closer to the mark, then?' she continued, her voice lifting in her own certainty. 'Is that what you're worried about—that your reluctant bride has to be dragged kicking and screaming to the altar because she's being forced to marry you? Is that why you can't let her have a fitting, because the poor girl can't bear the thought of wearing the dress on her wedding day, let alone any other time? Because she can't bear the thought of marrying you?'

He spun towards her, reaching out, cold fury gathered like storm clouds in his eyes, the lines of his golden skin drawn and tight around his mouth. His hands clenched down on her upper arms like iron claws, manacles for her arms, pinning her to the spot with a white-hot grip.

'You think your Paolo knows everything? Obviously he could not or you would not be here.'

'Wha—? What do you mean?'

'You really want to meet my bride? You so desperately want this fitting?'

She swallowed, tasting his fury on her tongue, swirling in the heated fog of his proximity. Yet even in a rage she felt his raw sexuality reach out for her.

Even in her fear she felt her own body react, her breasts achingly firm, her thighs soften and pulse within.

She battled to focus on his words when his lips were so close. Too close. She could bury herself in his heat, lose herself in his power.

He could make it happen and she would be powerless to stop him.

She wouldn't want to stop him.

She wouldn't even try to stop him.

'Well?' he demanded, dragging her thoughts back into focus. 'You want this fitting?'

She sucked in a breath too low on oxygen and too highly charged with the scent of him and tried to forget how much he affected her. 'All she needs is to try on the dress. Just once. That's all. And then I'll be happy.'

He scoffed. 'Then you'll be happy?'

Her chin kicked up, reclaiming some measure of defiance. 'Just one fitting. It's not too much to ask, surely?'

'Okay,' he said, almost discarding her as he let go his grip and wheeled away. Two strides on he turned back, the fury in his eyes replaced with something else—*boldness*? 'You win. You get your fitting.'

At last. She let go a deep breath she'd been holding and rubbed her arms where the touch of him lingered like a brand. She would finally get the fitting she'd been asking for, then she could complete the dress and get on the next flight out of here. It wouldn't be soon enough. 'So when? How soon can you arrange it?'

'Right now.'

There was no way she would miss the opportunity. 'About time. Would it be best to take the dress there?'

'No need for that. We can do it right here.'

'What do you mean—you'll bring her here?'

'No,' he said, the spark in his eyes taking on a victorious gleam. 'You wanted a fitting with the bride—you've got one.'

'But I don't understand.'

'So put it on.'

'What?'

'Put-the-dress-on!'

CHAPTER SIX

'No!' COLD fear crashed over her, a drenching wave that left logic spluttering in its wake. 'This has to be some kind of sick joke.'

His eyebrows lifted in response, his mouth curling dangerously into a bare grin that held no trace of humour. He took a step closer. 'You will make a beautiful bride.'

She shook her head, inching backwards as she kept her eyes fixed on him, willing him to keep his distance as her mind battled for reason.

He moved closer still.

'You're just trying to scare me, because I insisted on this fitting. You're just trying to get back at me.' She felt the worktable behind her, clutching on to it with tight fingers for support, praying for its solidity and strength to supplement her own.

'Are you going to try it on?'

'No, of course not.'

He stopped just inches away, looking down at her, and she waited for the moment when he would reach out and touch her, searing her again with his hands.

It was crazy. What he was saying was crazy, yet still the anticipation of his touch threatened to wipe out logical thought. And she needed to think straight, needed to harness every shred of reason that she could muster in order to fight her way out of his onslaught.

'You were the one who insisted on a fitting.'

'It's not my dress.'

'Isn't it? Then whose measurements do you think were provided to you? That dress was made to fit you like a glove. That dress was made for you.'

'How?' she asked even as the realisation hit her—they'd taken her measurements her first morning here. *She'd let them take them.* 'You tricked me. You said those were so they could make some sort of gift. You lied to me.'

He shook his head. 'I did not lie. Your traditional Jebbai garments have been made for you. I just did not tell you all of the truth.'

'This is mad. I'm not your bride. I won't be your bride. You can't make me.'

'I won't need to. You'll come to me willingly.'

She laughed, her tension betrayed in the short, fractured sound. 'Now you kid yourself. Why the hell would I do that?'

'Because,' he said, curling one hand around her neck, while the other snaked its way around her waist, pulling her close and extinguishing the space between them, 'you want me.'

She fought the pressure of his hands, not allowing herself to be collected as easily as he might wish. 'In your dreams.'

'I do dream, as it happens,' he said, his voice low and close to her ear, so that his breath curled against her skin, the sensation assailing her senses. 'And I dream of you, in my bed, under me, on top of me, bucking with me. Every way I dream of you and your eyes flashing blue as you explode in my arms.'

Her breath stuck fast in her throat as his lips caressed the skin under her ear while the very same pictures played wide-screen in her mind.

It wasn't just her then.

The attraction she'd felt, the pull, the magnetism— if what he said was true it wasn't just one-sided. He felt it too, this allure, this desire.

Clothing faded to insignificance as she was dragged into contact with him, from her chest to her thighs, and, for all the protection they gave her, her clothes might not have been there. His arousal pressed firm and hard into her belly, proof of his own attraction and upping the gears on her own need. Involuntarily she squirmed against him, driven more by passion than by common sense.

He uttered something in Arabic, something primal and guttural, a low roar that spoke of his own desires, as he lowered his head, meshing his mouth with hers.

Her senses blurred in the rush of blood, the bloom of hotness that came at the touch of his lips, as his mouth moved over hers. *Intoxicating.* How could one mouth feel so persuasive, so magical?

The urge to comply with the sweet demands of his lips was almost irresistible, the urge to let her own mouth open and blossom under his overwhelming. He tasted of intensity and power, of the timeless desert sands, and he tasted so right. He felt so right. Her body was already preparing itself for more, wanting more.

But he wasn't right.

He was wrong.

Wrong about her—wrong for her—just plain wrong. And she would be making the mistake of her life to give in to his sensual onslaught.

How could she believe anything he said or did? This was a man who'd brought her to Jebbai under false pretences. This was a man who'd got her here by claiming he was marrying another, only to think he could claim her for his bride.

This was a man who had lost his grip on reality.

And she would not be part of his fantasy!

She wrenched back her head, fighting off the band of his arm around her neck, pushing him away at his shoulders.

'No,' she breathed, her mouth dodging his searching lips. 'Let me go.'

He caught her hands in his, trapping her forearms against his chest. 'You want me, don't try to deny it.'

'No. I don't want you,' she insisted, her voice defiant, even though she knew she was hardly telling the whole truth. 'Why would I? I have a boyfriend.'

Strangely he smiled. It was the last thing she'd expected and his cool reaction to her words stilled her fight.

'Ah, of course. Paolo.' In her motionless state he transferred one wrist to join the other. With his free hand he drew a slow line from her forehead to her chin. 'The newspapers seemed to suggest he was more than just a *boyfriend*, though. Wasn't there talk of marriage between you?'

Her veins turned to ice even as his fingers seemed to sear her soul. How would he know that? Just how long had he been watching her?

'All right,' she said, putting aside the complications of her relationship with Paolo in the disturbing warmth generated by Khaled's touch. 'Yes, I have a fiancé. And if I'm going to marry anyone, I'd prefer it to be him.'

He laughed, sudden and loud and as if he was truly enjoying himself. Yet there was unmistakably a hard edge she heard there too.

'Tell me, then,' he asked, 'do you think Paolo will rush to your rescue? Do you think he would marry you himself, just to save you from me? Is your lover that much of a hero?'

'Of course he would marry me,' she maintained, stiffening further in his arms, certain that, for all his recent and inexplicable inability to commit, he would never let her suffer the indignity of a forced marriage to anyone, let alone someone like Sheikh Khaled. 'And he will, just as soon as I get out of this place.'

She kicked her chin up defiantly. So it wasn't exactly the truth—Khaled didn't need to know that, and Paolo *had* said that they would work out their differences on her return. But if it brought Khaled to his senses, so much the better.

He paused and frowned, and something indefinable intruded into his dark eyes. 'You love him that much you would believe that?' he asked, his dark, clouded eyes searching hers.

The sudden tender note in his voice took her by surprise. Did he really care how much she felt for Paolo? 'I... Of course—'

He didn't wait for her to finish stumbling over her sentence. He let her go, lifting his hands from her and stalking away, raking one hand through his hair.

'He won't marry you,' he said softly.

She wasn't sure she'd heard right. 'Pardon?'

'He won't marry you.' This time louder so there was no mistaking his words.

'You can't know that,' she accused, her voice amazingly steady while all the time her mind screamed, *How do you know?* How could he sound so sure, so certain? There was no way he could know something like that.

His eyes told her he did.

Warning bells sounded in her head. 'What's this all about?' she asked, trying to connect the dots between Khaled's crazy intention to marry her and Paolo's deep-seated resentment. She wasn't sure what it meant, but somehow there was a connection. There had to be. 'Why me? Why did you pick on me to be your bride?'

He shrugged. 'I saw a picture of you. I heard about your reputation. Everything I learned about you fascinated me. I had to meet you. And when I met you, in the salon, I knew you were the one for me.'

She surveyed him coolly. 'That's too unbelievable for words.'

'Why? Don't you believe in love at first sight? It happened to my father. Why shouldn't the same thing happen to me?'

'Because unlike your mother, I already have a boyfriend. I'm not looking for a husband.'

'Paolo won't marry you because he can't.'

Something inside her snapped. She'd had enough. She threw her hands up in the air in exasperation. She didn't want any more of his mind games. She didn't need them. Now that he'd let her go she had better things to do with her time—like pack her suitcase and get out of there.

'I don't have to listen to this. I don't know what you think you know and I don't really care. I'm leaving.'

She turned for the door and his words came after her as sharp as a dagger. 'Didn't you hear me? It's not possible for him to marry you.'

'I'm not listening,' she said, shaking her head as she reached for the workshop door to slam behind her. 'I don't care.'

She gave the door one hell of a swing, thinking her energies could have been much better directed at connecting her fist with one particularly arrogant sheikh's jaw, but there was no resounding slam, no satisfying conclusion. She turned, growling in frustration, only to see him right behind her, blocking the space the door should have filled.

'Don't you want to know why?'

She put her hands over her ears as she headed for her bedroom. 'No. I don't want to hear what you think you know. Don't you understand? I just want to get out of here. I just want to get away from you!'

'Then you should care,' he said, nonchalantly tracing her steps. 'Because it's obvious that, for someone apparently in love with you, he hasn't been totally honest.'

That got her attention! She swivelled around where she stood, buried in the walk-in wardrobe, her suitcase in hand, already in flight. Just her luck that when she finally got to enjoy a dressing room large enough to swing a suitcase, she would have been more than happy to hit a few walls, or one particular sheikh, just for effect.

'Oh, that's rich, coming from you.' She flipped open the suitcase on the floor, started tearing clothes from hangers and flinging them in while the prick of tears stung her eyes, blurring her vision. But there was no way she was giving in to them. No way. 'What would you know about honesty? You've lied to me from day one.'

'But I never pretended to be in love with you.'

Her frantic movements stilled, her hands midway to the next item, as the fury inside her reached meltdown. 'You're mad!' she said, dragging the shirt free from its hanger at last. 'You must be, to think that I would stay here to be your bride. To even talk about love in such circumstances is a joke. I don't want you as a husband and I certainly don't want your love.'

She collected up the few remaining items from the shelves and tossed them on top of everything else before pushing past him to get to her bathroom and gather up her toiletries. She jammed the zipper bag on top and then bundled the whole pile to somehow fit the suitcase's confines.

'Where do you think you're going?'

'Where do you think? I'm going home.' She flipped out the case's handle, set it right side up on its wheeled base and puffed out her chest defiantly. 'And then I'm going to marry Paolo.'

She pushed past him, unsure of how exactly she was going to get to the airport and how long she'd have to wait when she got there for a flight, but determined to get out now anyway.

'That's *after* his divorce comes through, I take it.'

She kept walking with barely a hitch, her heeled sandals clicking on the cool tiled floor, suitcase rolling behind. 'Well, if that's your trump card,' she said without raising her voice, knowing he was still close enough to hear every word, 'you just blew it. I'm afraid you've got the wrong Paolo. My fiancé has never been married.'

'Oh, he never shared that piece of information with you, then?'

'On the contrary. He had nothing to share. Like I said, you've got the wrong Paolo.'

'Paolo Eduardo Mancini? Married an English student, Helene Elizabeth Grainger, in Paris on March twenty-fifth twelve years ago. Funny that he'd never share that news with you, his lover, his fiancée.'

Okay, so what that he had Paolo's name right? She bit down on her bottom lip and forced herself further along the hallway. No way was she going to show him he was rattling her. It couldn't be true. It just couldn't.

Although it could explain why Paolo had been so cagey...

No!

She trusted Paolo. She had no reason at all to doubt him. Whereas she had no reason to trust Khaled. No reason at all.

'You'll have to do better than that, I'm afraid,' she tossed over her shoulder with a wave of her free hand as she kept walking.

'Then maybe you'd appreciate seeing the wedding video? Or perhaps the photographs. I have an extensive collection.'

Video? Photographs? This time her steps faltered as the air evaporated in her lungs.

'Why should I believe you?' She didn't turn and her voice was barely more than a croak. Surely it couldn't be true? And if it was, why hadn't Paolo told her?

All this time!

All this time they'd been dating and seeing each other and not once, even just once, had he intimated that he was already married, that he already had a wife. Why the hell wouldn't he have admitted to something like that? *Dammit*—he should have told her!

'In the end it's not about what you believe. It's about the truth. Your *fiancé* has already been married for twelve years.'

She squeezed her eyes shut as her head dipped to

her chest. 'Then I want to call him,' she said before sucking air deep into her lungs and looking back at him over her shoulder. 'Now!'

Five minutes later she was holding on to the receiver in Khaled's office, clutching the phone with white-knuckled fingers, waiting while the phone rang in an apartment somewhere in New York. She couldn't sit, nervous energy wouldn't let her limbs relax.

She had to stand, shifting impatiently from one foot to the other as she waited for the call to be picked up halfway around the globe, all the while trying to ignore the arrogant Jebbai ruler who sprawled unconscionably in the well-worn leather armchair opposite. He obviously had no trouble relaxing and that only added to her fears. The one hope that he'd back down on his crazy claims at her insistence on phoning Paolo drizzled away. He must be so certain that what he was saying was true.

She turned her back on his smug demeanour and glanced at her watch. What time was it in New York now? Some time in the night—he had to be there—she had to discover the truth now—or she didn't know what she'd do.

Eventually the phone was picked up and Paolo answered. 'Yes?' came his voice, thick with sleep and husky as if he'd tumbled straight out of bed to answer the phone. Something squeezed in her heart as she clamped her eyes shut, trying to staunch the flow of tears still so closely threatening. She knew that voice, had once rejoiced in it as he'd held her in his arms, had whispered to her how beautiful she was and that she was the most important person in the world to him.

But now it wasn't love she felt, love to warm and sustain her and hold her true. Now it was icy panic clamping her inside, compressing her last frantic hopes.

'Who is it?' More alert now, she could tell.

'Paolo,' she whispered, her voice set to break.

'Sapphy, *bella*. Is that you? What's wrong? Has something happened?'

The once oft-used term of endearment sliced a cold path through her with ruthless efficiency. If what Khaled said was true, she'd never been his darling, his sweetheart. Someone had held that place long before her.

'Sapphy? Are you still in Jebbai? What's Khaled done?' There was fear in his voice too, laced heavily with alarm. Was this just the normal concern of a person woken in the middle of the night to what could be devastating news, or did his reaction signal a deeper dread?

She swallowed back on a sob. 'Nothing's wrong,' she lied, feeling her whole world splitting apart as easily as fabric snipped at the edge and ripped in two. 'Just tell me one thing…' She hesitated, knowing that this moment was about to change her life, change all her perceptions about living and love, and teach her about betrayal. This moment would be the start of her new life, in whatever form that took.

'Is it true—are you married? Do you have a wife?'

Silence met her questions, a damning silence that fractured whatever threads of hope remained intact. They were gone, shattered, smashed in his soundless affirmation of the truth.

'It's true, then,' she said on a sniff. 'You should have told me.'

'Sapphy, listen to me. I couldn't tell you—'

Even though his silence had already screamed the truth, his words cemented the facts with a cold, hard reality that shook her.

'I have nothing more to say to you,' she uttered with finality, her voice as chilled as her heart. 'Goodbye, Paolo.'

'Sapphy, listen to me—'

She dropped the receiver back onto the cradle. 'Goodbye, Paolo,' she whispered, shivering now, her arms hugged closely to her chest as the shock of deep sudden loss took hold.

Strong arms surrounded her and pulled her close. For a moment she wanted to struggle—what was this? The victorious barbarian staking his claim? But she sensed none of that with his warmth. Instead she felt compassion, even some kind of understanding, and she sagged gratefully into him, welcoming the solace and comfort he offered.

His strong heartbeat thumped loud in his chest, its rhythm steady and firm and as rock-solid as the man holding her.

'It's okay,' he whispered against her hair. His lips brushed her scalp in the barest of kisses and the warmth from the contact radiated down through her as her breathing steadied, her heart rate calming to match his.

And it hit her then.

Her life hadn't changed when she'd discovered the truth about Paolo. It had changed the moment Khaled had stepped inside the Milan salon. He'd been the catalyst, the trigger that had turned her life upside down.

When Khaled had kissed her that first time in the workroom, he'd forced her to face up to her ambivalence in her feelings for Paolo. She could never have betrayed someone she loved deeply by falling into the arms of another man. Now it had been Khaled again who'd proved her relationship had been a sham from the beginning.

Whatever his motives were for doing it she had no idea, but she certainly didn't have to thank him for it.

It was time to regain control of her life.

She peeled herself away from his chest, aware of his reluctance to let her go and dipping her head so she could wipe away the traces of tears before he could see them.

'I'm sorry you had to find out that way.'

'Are you?' she snapped. His gentle words did nothing to ease her pain and everything to cement her resolve. 'It seemed to me you were only too happy to throw that knowledge in my face.'

'It was time you knew the truth.'

'Why? What does it have to do with you anyway? Did you think I would be so devastated by the news that I would happily fall in with your crazy plans to marry you? I've just rid myself of one lying man. Why the hell would I launch myself straight into the arms of another?'

His jaw looked as if he was grinding his teeth together. Then he whispered, low and menacingly, 'Never put me in the same category as Paolo.'

'Why the hell not? Why are you doing this? Paolo said you two had been involved in some feud years ago. I told him he was being crazy, that no one probably even cared any more. But you do, don't you? You care so much it's like a poison in your system. Tell me, what did he do? Why do you hate him so much?'

Anger set the planes of his face hard and cold. 'You're upset,' he said, his voice revealing a barely controlled fury.

So he was mad, good for him. It was *nothing* to how she was feeling.

'Damned right, I'm upset,' she said. 'And I'll stay upset until I get out of this place. You don't have to become the barbarian. For the most part you appear to be a civilised man. You have no need to act like some petty despot. And if you have any respect for me at all, if you think anything of me, you have to respect my wishes. Let me go. I have to go.'

He looked down at her, the depths of his dark eyes swirling, his brow knotted, and her hopes lifted. Was he relenting in his mad desire to make her his wife? Had he realised he'd inflicted enough damage on her already?

'I can't let you go.'

Fury blasted through her. 'Then I'll go in spite of you. I'll find some other way of getting to the airport and I'll go anyway. Because I won't stay here.'

She stormed her way to her suitcase propped up near the door and grabbed purposefully at the handle.

'You're not going anywhere.'

'I'm not staying here. I'm definitely not marrying you.'

'So you keep saying, but that changes nothing. You cannot leave Jebbai now.'

'You can't keep me here. I want to go home.'

'But not today,' he said. 'Not for at least twenty-four hours.'

'I have to get away,' she said, half-demanding, half-pleading.

'You have no choice, as it turns out,' he snapped, his voice cold and imperious again. 'The airport is closed.'

CHAPTER SEVEN

'YOU'RE lying.' Her voice seemed surprisingly level under the circumstances. 'This is just some pathetic attempt to keep me here. But it won't work. I'm leaving.'

'Unfortunately it's true. Insurgents from neighbouring Jamalbad have been stirring up trouble along the border. This is the second such infraction in a few weeks—the first happened while we were *en route* from Milan. It seems someone thought that my absence then was an opportune time to stir up trouble.'

She thought back to the plane flight, his sudden disappearance, the urgent discussions going on around the communications equipment.

'I remember,' she said. 'Yet in spite of that danger, you still brought me here.'

'I would never have brought you here if I'd thought it was serious. My guards believed they'd dealt with the problem. It now appears they missed the ringleaders. They've still been out there, stirring up trouble. We've closed the airport as a precautionary measure.'

'For an entire day?'

He shrugged. 'It is best to be prudent—perhaps it will be closed for less.'

She looked ruefully down at the suitcase and let go

91

of the handle. It was like letting go of a lifeline. He'd told her she would be safe here. Now she couldn't get away even when she wanted to.

And how she wanted to.

She wanted to be as far away from this desert ruler as possible. Her previous life had never seemed calm—the fashion industry was madness as well as maddening, but compared to the way her feelings and emotions were being tossed about now it was a cakewalk.

She didn't want to stay near Khaled. If his scheming methods to get her here weren't frightening enough, his quiet declaration that he didn't have to force her to marry him and that she would come to him of her own accord scared her even more.

He was kidding himself! Not that she wanted to hang around to prove his theory wrong. But neither did she want to stay and be subjected to the pull of his fiery magnetism.

She couldn't trust herself to resist it.

'I'm sorry,' he said, 'but I promise you will be safe. That's why I came to see you today. I wanted you to hear it from me, to assure you that we are dealing with the problem and that Jebbai will soon be returned to its former peaceful existence.'

'And what of my former peaceful existence?' she said. 'When will I be returned to that?'

She looked so fragile right then, her blue eyes foggy with vulnerability and defeat, and he felt her anguish deep inside, in a place he'd long thought shrivelled and empty.

She did that to him. Touched him in ways no one ever had. Why else would he have risked his whole plan by revealing the truth so soon? Her constant goads, her insistent demands, they had been bad enough—nobody had ever defied him the way she did. But it was the way she seemed so desperate to return to her deceitful lover that had forced him over the edge of reason.

So he'd spilled his intention to take her as his bride much earlier than he'd planned and in doing so he'd threatened the entire scheme.

But maybe this way was better. Maybe now he would secure a far more effective payback.

Already he'd exacted a measure of revenge upon his former foe. He'd smelt the fear coming down the phone line as clearly as one felt the blast-furnace heat of a Jebbai midsummer day. Half a world away Paolo would know that this was his doing, he would know that he had brought this on with his own precipitous actions so long ago. He would wear the guilt like a heavy burden he could never shrug off. He would bear the pain forever.

As for Sapphire? Her anguish at her so-called fiancé's betrayal was palpable. He'd felt her despair like a knife thrust under his ribs; it touched him deep inside and instinctively, *bizarrely*, he wanted to make it better.

He had thought it would be easy—to take the woman of the man he hated as easily as stealing one of his possessions. Yet this woman was no cold chattel, no inanimate property. She was warm, and human and so responsive.

And he wanted her.

Oh, how he wanted her.

He wanted to feel more of her responsiveness, more of her body curling into his, more of her body melding with his until she was part of him, until they were part of each other.

And he wanted her now.

Even now, when she looked so lost and lonely, the urge to possess her, to ease her pain by obliterating any trace of Paolo in her mind and stamping his own claim on her, was almost primal.

He moved closer to her then, her hands clasped nervously in front of her like a young schoolgirl unsure of her next step in the world or where it would take her. If he had any say in the matter, that next step would take her straight to him, but this time it was up to her.

This time she would decide.

He wouldn't take her. She would give herself to him.

And then his victory over Paolo would be complete.

He lifted her chin with his hand and watched her large blue eyes reluctantly rise to meet his, the dampness in them rendering her long lashes heavy and dark.

'I will take you to the airport,' he said. 'When it reopens and when it is safe, I will take you there myself.'

He watched her nervous swallow, followed the movement in her throat, and fought the urge to drop his mouth and cover the pearly skin there with his lips.

'You'll let me go?' Her breath was choppy and hesitant; her bottom lip plumped and reddened with the tracks from her teeth.

'If that's what you want.'

Her eyes grew wide with hope and expectation and he accepted the challenge. He would make it his duty to change those expectations before it was time for her to leave.

'If that's what you *really* want.'

'Of course it's what I really want.'

'Then that's what will happen,' he asserted. 'We have a deal.'

'How…' she started unsuccessfully. She licked her lips as if searching for the courage. 'How do I know I can trust you?'

'I assure you my word is my honour—' he smiled when he noticed her sceptical expression '—although I understand you may not entirely agree. But perhaps you are right. Perhaps in deference to your concerns we should seal our bargain. We could shake hands—' his free hand surrounded her own, squeezing it reassuringly on feeling her electric reaction '—or we could seal our agreement with something much, *much* more satisfying…'

He saw the panic flare in her eyes, felt her instant reaction for flight as she pulled back. 'Just a kiss,' he promised. 'No more than that.'

He tugged her gently closer with one hand, tilting her towards him while he directed her chin with the other, until his mouth slanted over hers. He felt the shudder move through her as his lips meshed with hers, as if her internal resolve was being rocked and tested. He felt her sigh into the kiss, as if knowing she had no choice.

And she hadn't.

She might as well get used to it.

His tongue traced the line of her lips, tasting, examining, cajoling, and at the precise moment, at the tiniest hint he felt she was responding, he pulled away, letting go of his hold on her in the same instant.

Her eyelids batted open, her cheeks were flushed and her lips red and plumped.

It was enough for now.

He could have continued, God, but it had taken every shred of control to pull himself away when all he wanted to do was bury himself deep inside her. And he would. He would erase from her mind all thought of Paolo, every last memory of his lovemaking, every last aching pain of his deceit. He would have her. But not yet. Not just yet.

He would not take her.

He would make her come to him.

'So, do we have a deal?'

She reeled, knowing that once again he'd taken her to that place where she forgot herself, forgot who he was and even forget that she wanted to get away from there. How did he do that? And why did she feel so cheated that he'd stopped?

'Sure.' Her voice came too soft and sultry for her liking, so she tried again, searching for more resolve. *'Definitely,'* she said, adding a nod of her head for emphasis. 'You'll take me to the airport when it re-opens.'

He looked down at her, half smiling. 'If that's what you really want.'

'Oh,' she said, 'I want.'

I think.

She dropped her eyes so there was no chance he'd catch even a glimmer of her inner turmoil, and moved to collect her case, doing her best to distract herself from wherever her thoughts were about to take her. She'd return to her room. Think about practicalities. Focus on doing her packing a little more thoroughly.

And forget all about uncertainty.

'One more thing,' he said as she reached the door. 'I must attend a meeting with the desert tribes this evening. It will mean an overnight trip. I'll be leaving later today.'

Surprise mingled with relief mingled with disappointment. She wouldn't see him again before he returned to take her to the airport. Their time together before she left would be limited to a short ride in his limousine, if that. She should be happier about that, given the experience he'd put her through, surely?

'Is it safe for you to travel away from Hebra, under the circumstances?'

One of his eyebrows arched. 'Now you are concerned for my safety? You do surprise me. A moment ago I think you would quite happily have thrown my body out for carrion.'

She blinked, her lips tightening. 'If I show concern it's for the poor people you will no doubt drag along with you on this desert sojourn. It's their safety that concerns me.'

His lips turned up in the barest smile. 'Of course. But it's perfectly safe. I'm headed to the opposite end of the country.'

'Yet you thought it was safe when you brought me here. That doesn't say much for your risk-assessment analysis.'

'I assure you, I've assessed the risks,' he said, his eyes narrowing to a dark gleam, 'and I'm willing to take them on.'

Heat flooded her senses. She'd experienced enough of his double meanings to realise there was little doubt his words were aimed squarely at her.

But he had no chance. In one day, no more than two at the outside, she'd be gone. There was no way now that she could fall any further under his spell. Her own risk assessment told her she was just about home free.

'In that case,' she said, lifting her chin and finally feeling as if she was turning today's events around, 'I only hope you're not disappointed.'

'How could I be disappointed,' he asked, 'when you're coming with me?'

CHAPTER EIGHT

'No,' SHE said without a moment's hesitation. 'I don't think that's such a good idea.'

Whatever her see-sawing emotions were telling her, her brain was still screaming that she should get out of Jebbai as fast as possible and, failing that, to stay right away from Khaled. On that basis, going into the desert with him overnight was simply not an option.

'Why not,' he asked, 'when you have seen little or nothing of my country? You've buried yourself in that workroom. This would be the perfect chance to explore wider afield, before you return home.'

'Go with you, into the desert, when only minutes ago you were telling me I was to be your bride? You must think I'm mad or stupid to wander off into the desert with you when all I want to do is go home.'

'You will go home, if you wish. I gave you my word.'

'You got me here under false pretences. You lied to me all the way. You even let me believe in a bride that was an entire fabrication. I have to wonder what your word is really worth.'

He looked up, surprised. 'I'd hardly describe you as an entire fabrication. Besides, I thought we'd sealed that particular deal.'

'That was your concept of sealing a deal, not mine,' she threw at him.

'I see,' he said. 'You think we should seal the deal with something more…' his eyes took on a predatorial gleam '…*comprehensive?*'

Heat suffused her skin in an instant, a heavy, longing pooling low down in her belly. *'More comprehensive.'* The images his words conjured up sprang ready formed into her mind. A shock of tangled limbs; his smooth, sweat-slickened skin slipping over hers; his mouth, hot and hungry at her breast…

She forced the pictures back down, all of them, back to where they couldn't betray her any more than the hardened peaks of her nipples already did. It was bad enough he was so painfully arrogant without her body responding to his taunts.

'Don't expect me to sleep with you, simply to get out of the country.'

'I don't,' he said, swooping down to pick up her case. 'When you sleep with me I expect it to be for much more basic reasons.' He caught the look of shock on her face and smiled. 'Of course, I meant *if* you sleep with me.'

His instant correction did nothing to reassure her.

'I… I'll stay in the palace.'

'No. You're my responsibility. I won't know you're safe unless I take you with me.'

'I'll be safer here, surely. There are rebels, you said, insurgents out there somewhere. Why wouldn't I be better off here?'

'This palace is my home. I have doubts they could get this far, but if someone is after me then this is the first place they'll look. I won't leave you here alone.'

'I have Azizah.'

'And Saleem...'

Mention of his cousin stilled her protests. Saleem would hardly accept the role of her protector. He didn't like her, no matter how much she tried to stay out of his way and not upset him. The resentment was there, the mistrust clear in his eyes. He gave every impression that he hated her, but why? What had she ever done to him? And did she really want to endure his cold glares for two days alone?

'Wouldn't Saleem go with you?'

He shook his head. 'He has other matters to attend to. He must stay here.'

'Oh.' Saleem was staying in the palace. That put a completely different slant on things.

'You still don't like him?'

'I don't know—he just makes me feel uncomfortable, unsettled.'

'Saleem is my cousin. You should not feel that way.'

'I know. I just don't feel that I can trust him.'

'Like you don't trust me?'

Not like that at all. Khaled's simple question came with a simple answer that only complicated her thoughts. Her mistrust of Saleem was whole and entire and every cell in her body reacted in the same adverse way to his presence. He made her cringe, he made her flesh creep. She just didn't want to be anywhere around him.

Her mistrust of Khaled was completely different. She doubted his motives, she resented his arrogance and his duplicity in getting her here for reasons still not clear to her, but it was her body that she mistrusted the most. It was her body that reached out for him at the very same time her brain repelled him. It was her body that wanted him.

And she couldn't trust herself to deny him. Maybe staying in the palace with Saleem was the lesser of two evils after all, even though the thought chilled her to the bone.

Khaled didn't wait for her answer.

'Then I will not let you stay. You will come with me.'

Panic welled up inside her. 'But—'

'Sapphire,' he said, the sound of his voice strangely soothing, like a parent convincing a child, 'it's only for one night after all. What can possibly happen in one night?'

In less than two hours they were on their way out of the city and heading into the desert, the narrow strip of bitumen their only link to modern life. Sapphy travelled in the first Range Rover with Khaled choosing to drive. Half a dozen staff followed in the second.

The terrain at first was much like it had been driving into Hebra, stark, sandy flats broken by the occasional thorny plant, the air dry and clear, but gradually the landscape changed and the sand formed dunes, low and barely distinguishable at first, growing higher as they headed deeper and deeper into the desert.

Sculpted by the incessant winds, the red sand-dunes billowed all around them, creeping over the road in places and making the going tough. She sat quietly alongside Khaled as he drove, avoiding talk as far as possible and letting the landscape speak to her.

She couldn't regret coming here. Even after all that had happened, she'd learned so much visiting Jebbai, experiencing palace life in Hebra, cool and insulated and heady with the ever-present scent of incense; visiting the city souks with Azizah and the colourful market stalls with their wares both simple and exquisite. Even his mother's garden at the palace had been an experience that had fed into her psyche, enriching her experience of this country.

And Khaled? She looked over to him, his profile as majestic as the country he ruled, his strong features sculpted in his face like the lines carved by the wind in the dunes. With the white sleeves of his shirt rolled up to his elbows, his lean forearms worked at the wheel over the uneven territory and the occasional sand drift with strength and skill. Even some part of Khaled, whether it was his power, his arrogance or his dark and dangerous eyes, would feed into her work, she was sure. There was no way she would be able to divorce him from the experience.

He looked over, snaring her gaze.

'You're very quiet,' he said. 'Are you finding the journey too tiring?'

'Not at all,' she answered truthfully. Khaled had been right. She'd concentrated so much on completing the wedding dress that she'd barely been out of the workroom. In many ways it was exciting to be out of the palace and away from the city. 'Jebbai is much bigger than it looks on the map.'

He smiled, showing his even white teeth. 'We are

one of the smaller independent states, it is true, though the desert certainly makes the country seem much larger. There is more to see in terms of civilisation to the south, where the oil fields are situated. Here it is very empty, apart from the occasional tribe.'

'Well, at least you have four-wheel drives to get around these days. Beats the heck out of doing it all by camel.'

'Is that experience talking, or supposition?'

'Of course I've ridden on camels, lots of times.' She brushed her fringe out of her eyes. 'Nothing to it.'

He looked quickly over at her again but this time as if he didn't believe a word she said.

'Really. There are loads of camels in Australia, out in the outback. Leftovers gone wild from the eighteen-hundreds when they used them for transport. Now they catch them and the handlers bring them into the cities and use them to take kids for rides at the beach or at the annual shows. It makes a change from pony rides.

'Our nanny used to take us all to one of the beaches every year for an outing and we'd have a ride together. Opal, our older sister, loved the ponies the best. But with Ruby, my twin sister, and me, it was always the camels.'

'I'm impressed,' he said, a note of approval creeping into his voice. 'You're quite a multi-talented woman.'

She pressed her lips together and shook her head. 'Okay, you can laugh. But it was fun anyway.'

'Who said I'm laughing?' he said with all seriousness. 'You just never know when a skill like camel riding will come in handy.'

Behind her sunglasses she rolled her eyes, before turning them back to the endless dunes. 'Sure,' she said, dismissing him yet secretly pleased that in just one small way she'd managed to surprise him. He seemed a different person when they could touch on neutral topics, when whatever grievances he brought to their other dealings could be put aside.

It was at least twenty minutes before either of them spoke again. The road had all but disappeared under the drifting sands and her seat was getting less comfortable, the bumps were getting more pronounced and she was generally sick of the vehicle's grinding progress through the dunes.

She reached for her bottle of water and took a swig. 'How far now?'

'We'll be stopping soon.'

'We're nearly there?'

'Wait,' he said, the unexpected smile on his face warming her. 'I think you're going to like this.'

It wasn't long before she found out what he meant. They pulled into a relatively flat area, really no more than a space between dunes and dominated by an ancient and squat mud-brick building. It was the end of the road, literally, and what there was to like about it was anyone's guess.

The vehicles parked side by side under a lean-to and men started unloading the supplies.

'You might want to take this opportunity to freshen up,' Khaled suggested. He reached behind the front seat. 'And here, you might want to put this on. It will protect you from the sun and the sand.'

She took the bundle he held up to her. 'Why should I need this now?' she asked.

'Our journey is not quite over,' he said.

'What do you mean?'

He focused on something behind her. 'See for yourself,' he said.

A protesting bawl told her what she'd see before she turned.

'Camels!' she cried.

The man leading the first camels, his coiled-turban-framed face all leathery wrinkles from years of exposure to the desert sun, broke into a wide grin at her delight, revealing just three remaining teeth.

She reached up and stroked the nose of the first camel. It looked down at her, its thickly lashed, doe-like eyes considering her briefly, before lifting its head and letting out another loud bawl.

'You weren't kidding,' Khaled said, suddenly appearing at her side, his hand low on her back, the other stroking the neck of the camel. 'You really don't mind camels. Many people are not so keen, even afraid.'

'Camels get bad press,' she said, trying to ignore the pressure of his hand. He was barely touching her yet all her senses seemed to focus on that one point of contact, the warmth that built deep inside, pooling into longing. It was a struggle to pull herself back to the topic.

'But I've learned,' she continued, licking lips already losing moisture to the arid conditions, yet more so, as if edged with the heat emanating from him, the heat flowing from his gentle touch, 'that once you get to know them a little, it's clear their reputation has been unfairly earned.'

'Indeed? And do you think that observation might have its parallel with the human species? Do you similarly find that there are those people whose reputation has been unfairly attributed?'

He had to be kidding. She paused momentarily, considering him carefully and wondering if he was ever going to remove his hand. 'Your actions to date go far beyond mere reputation, Sheikh Khaled.'

'And does that then render me beyond redemption in your estimation?'

'When compared to camels, you mean?' She allowed herself a smile at his arrogance and shifted sideways out of his reach. 'Let's just say you're starting off from a much lower base.'

He threw his head back and laughed, the sound rich and mellow. She liked the sound of it when he laughed; she liked the effect it had on his features and the warmth it stirred inside her. Something let go in the muscles of his face and the harshness softened, the angles smoothed. She liked him like this, when he seemed less autocratic, more human.

A feeling akin to regret spiked her consciousness. If only things were different...

The camel bawled into her ear, spiking her out of her thoughts. What the hell was she thinking? Things weren't different. This guy had all but dragged her off to his desert kingdom with the intention of making her his wife. She was glad things weren't different. Now there was no way she could possibly like him.

So what that she'd had to accompany him out here? After tomorrow it wouldn't be an issue. She'd be gone. Long gone. He wouldn't see her for sand.

She felt his gaze settle upon her, hot and expectant, and she deliberately avoided it, focusing instead on the camels. She needed a distraction. She needed to think about something safe. Camels were just the ticket.

They were dromedaries, or one-humped, the same kind she was used to riding with her sisters on their childhood jaunts to the beach, but these wore different saddles. Instead of the double seat she remembered sharing with her sisters, this saddle was arranged over the hump, higher off the ground and more daunting. Not that she was about to admit that to Khaled.

'Which one is mine?' she asked, looking forward to the separation their mounts would bring. She could do with some distance from Khaled right now.

'This camel seems to like you. I think we will take this one.'

We will take this one? Impossible. That was so obviously a saddle built for one. If she had to share it with him, she'd be sitting literally in his lap, brushing against him, feeling his body rock against hers every step of the way. She swallowed.

'You mean, this one is for me.'

His lips curved into a grin. 'We're one camel short. You'll have to share with me.'

'Can't you get another one?'

He looked up at the sky. 'Too late. The track is

steep. We must leave now if we are to make the meeting place by nightfall.'

'But we won't both fit. There's nowhere for me to sit. It's not fair to the camel.'

'The camel can handle the slight addition of your weight. As to the rest, let me take care of that.'

Suddenly she wished she'd stayed back at the palace. Even the sullen moods of Saleem were less threatening than the prospect of spending time within Khaled's grasp.

'Can't I stay here? Wait for you to get back?'

'And miss the experience of a lifetime? A meeting with one of the few remaining Bedouin tribes—you would never forgive yourself for that, surely.'

Was he being obtuse or was he just teasing her? It wasn't missing the experience she was worried about. Couldn't he see that? Or did he see it too well?

She sucked in a breath, firing up her resolve. He hadn't got the better of her yet and she wasn't about to let him now. It would take more than a simple camel ride to make her change her view of Sheikh Khaled.

'Okay,' she said with a sense of bravado that surprised even herself. 'Let's do it.'

As it turned out, a few minutes later when they were ready to disembark, there was nothing simple about it. From the moment she'd been hauled into Khaled's arms she knew she was in for a rocky ride.

'Hold tight,' he warned her as the handler urged the camel upright, back legs first, threatening to plunge her forward into the sands if not for the steel-like bands of Khaled's arms surrounding her. Then the process was reversed as the camel raised itself on its front legs, forcing her bodily against him.

Then the five camels set off, with Khaled in the lead, padding their way over the soft desert sands. The side-by-side motion of the camel was familiar. The feel of his body so close to hers was not. She was nestled into the space between his thighs, pressed close to the wall of his chest, her head perilously close to his shoulder, feeling the friction between them increase with every step. His scent, woody and masculine, surrounded her, spiking subtly with the motion, adding to the cocktail of sensory impressions.

And there was no way she could hold herself aloof. There was no way she could keep her distance. If she wanted to stay on she had to cling to him, and cling tight.

Not that she was likely to fall off, not with the band of his arm circling her waist. Every breath she took, every rise of her chest brought his arm closer, tighter. But she dared not squirm. Already heat gathered low inside her, alluring, seductive. To wriggle in the cradle of his thighs would be to invite disaster.

'Are you not comfortable?' he asked, bending his head low to her ear. 'Maybe you should try to relax.'

Relax? Like that was on the cards. 'Why couldn't we take the cars? I would have thought that with four-wheel drives and helicopters, camels would have been a thing of the past.'

'Out here they still have some uses. There's an escarpment coming up. We could drive around but the camels will take the most direct route and save us hours of travel.'

'And helicopters?'

'Not half as much fun, wouldn't you agree?'

Her dark silence seemed to amuse him and his chuckle welled up, rippling through his chest. 'Besides, have you forgotten? The airport is closed. Such a shame.'

She gritted her teeth. 'A damn shame,' she muttered.

The ground became rockier. Pebbles took the place of sand and she became aware they were climbing, gradually at first, until they reached the escarpment and began the steep climb up the ancient track. Now she could see why they couldn't bring the cars. The narrow path was barely wide enough for a man, let alone a camel. A vehicle had no hope.

Below them the desert sands were spread out like a golden blanket, rippled and shadowed, warm and seductive in the fading light. It was beautiful and already she felt her life enriched, more textured by the experience.

The camel's movements became less rhythmic, more unpredictable as it ascended. Somewhere near the top of the escarpment, one plate-sized foot slid sideways on loose gravel and the camel lurched, jarring her out of Khaled's lap and threatening to launch her over the side, but his strong arms only tightened around her, reeling her back in close to him again.

She huddled close to his chest, waiting for her breathing to calm, her heart still racing from her narrow escape, but it was another rhythm that caught her attention. Outwardly he was so composed, so in charge. Yet inside she could feel his heart thumping wildly.

Had he been taken by surprise as well?

'Do not be afraid,' he whispered as she clung on to his arm. 'I would never let you fall. I would never let you get hurt.'

Tremors shook her body, though whether from relief or the impact of his words she couldn't be sure. For somehow she knew what he said was true.

'I'm okay,' she replied, thinking he might release his tight grip a fraction once he knew she was all right. But his arms stayed vice-like around her, even after they'd reached the summit and were finally nearing the collection of tents that made up the encampment. She couldn't wait to get down. The dust of a day's travel had worn into her skin and she was sure the smell of the camel had done likewise. But now she wouldn't have long to wait.

Small dark-haired children ran towards them, smiling and laughing, their long robes flapping around their bare shins and feet. A herd of goats looked up momentarily, checking out the latest distraction before losing interest.

A taller youth met the camels, his eyes alert and intelligent, his smile genuine. Excitement fired his features as he pulled on the nose ring of the lead camel and urged him to sit. Sapphy felt herself rocked forward as the camel dropped to its knees but Khaled's grip never let her fall. Then the camel was down. He released his hold enough for her to slip out of his grasp and onto the earth before he, too, dismounted.

'Majeed,' Khaled said, embracing the boy.

'Good day, Sheikh Khaled,' he replied formally, obviously working hard at his English. 'You have brought my new teacher?'

'Of course, Majeed. Didn't I promise?'

Moments later she noticed the youth leading away one of their fellow travellers. She wanted to ask Khaled about the exchange—she'd assumed their several accompanying riders were all guards—but she was surrounded by the young children, hanging on to her hands and chattering non-stop.

'You might want to clean up now,' he suggested to her, ruffling the children's hair as he steered her through the throng and towards the camp. 'Your bag will have been delivered already. I will show you to your tent.'

He turned back to the children and rattled off something fast in his language. They all scattered immediately, heading for the tents like shot from a gun.

'What did you say to them?'

'I told them to tell their mothers the doctor will be ready to see them shortly.'

'A doctor came with us? I thought those men were guards.'

'We had one guard with us, it's true. But guards won't do my people much good. They need practical help if they want to keep this way of life for as long as they can. They need medical help and immunisation clinics. It is much too far for them to travel into the cities for such luxuries.'

'Is that why you brought the teacher?'

He nodded. 'Exactly. The boy, Majeed, is very

bright. He has already surpassed his previous teacher's level. He needs new challenges and to learn new skills.'

'Couldn't he go to school in Hebra? Don't they have boarding-schools in Jebbai?'

'Of course. But then how could he help his family? He will go to university, when it is time and when his brothers are older. But his father needs him now and this way he can both study and help with his family.'

'I see,' she said, even though she didn't. Oh, it made sense all right. But this was a completely different side of Khaled. She was used to the ruthless, authoritarian side of him, the Khaled who acted out of anger, with no thought to the feelings of those he trampled with his unreasonable demands.

This was a different man. A real leader of his people, who ensured their ongoing existence in the style of life they had been accustomed to since ancient times. He could have forced them to abandon their way of life and move to the cities in the name of progress, simply by not supplying them with modern medicine and education. Yet he was ensuring the continued existence and preservation of their separate and special way of life. And from his reception here he was clearly well loved and respected as their leader.

How could someone who was so considerate and generous towards his people act so unreasonably towards her? It made no sense. No sense at all.

In the gathering dusk she noticed the women emerging from tents, their long robes flapping in the light breeze, babies in slings on their backs, many with young toddlers following in their wake.

They converged on a small tent set to one side, where one of the men who had travelled with them—the doctor, it was now clear—was setting up his equipment. It couldn't be an easy life for these people, always wandering and rarely settled, but they looked happy and healthy as they collected outside the tent, waiting for the doctor to attend to them.

'After you,' Khaled said and she realised he was holding open the tent for her. She stepped inside. It took a few seconds for her eyes to adjust to the lantern-lit interior and then her first reaction was to gasp.

The tent's interior bore no relation to its plain exterior. The floor was lined with carpets, woven and richly coloured. Curtains lined the walls, silks and gauzes softly draped in vivid jewel shades, and cushions lay scattered around, inviting and sumptuous. Perfumed candles scented the air, sweet and fragrant. Beyond an open silken partition she could just make out a large bed, presumably her bed, given what looked like her bag placed on top.

It was every little girl's fantasy. And despite all the dreams she'd had from way back to be a fashion designer, she could even believe it was hers. She'd grown up surrounded by luxury, been raised in the most exclusive boutique hotel in Australia, but this somehow went beyond mere fantasy. This was pure magic.

'Will you be comfortable here?'

She spun around slowly, trying to take it all in. 'Oh, yes. It's beautiful.'

His hand reached for her shoulder, stopping her right in front of him. His other hand tilted her chin. 'Though nowhere near as beautiful as you.'

Her breath caught as his face hovered above hers, his golden skin glowing and shadowed in the lamplight, a magic prince for a magic setting.

It could have been a fairy-tale.

Except she had no place in this story. She had already chosen her course. She would leave Jebbai, return to Milan, and before long all this would seem no more than a dream.

She raised one hand to his chest, uncertain of whether she was trying to stop him or merely giving in to the temptation of touching him again, of tasting his muscled torso with her fingers, of reading the strong beat of his heart.

The hand on her shoulder moved to cover hers, wrapping her fingers in his. His eyes still locked on hers, he lifted it from his chest and pressed the palm of her hand to his mouth. She sucked in air as his warm lips, his heated breath danced over her skin, as the merest trace of his tongue spread liquid warmth coursing through her.

'And now,' he said, his voice low and thick, 'relax a while. The women will help you. I have business to discuss with the men and then we will dine together.'

Women? She looked around to see two women near the bed unpacking her bag. Unfamiliar blue fabric shot with gold floated over one woman's hands. Sapphy frowned.

'That's not my bag,' she said, stepping towards the partition. 'It can't be.'

'You will find it is,' Khaled responded.

'But none of this…' The women moved aside while she checked the bag—it looked like hers, yet nothing inside was familiar. She dug her hands through the gossamer fabrics, the golden tassels and belts, the heavier cloaks. She didn't own these things. Yet, underneath everything else, there was her toiletry bag. It didn't make sense.

And yet all of a sudden it did.

Icy realisation filled her veins. This was just the sort of thing she should have expected from someone who had frustrated her at every move. She turned, barely able to restrain the mounting hostility within.

'What have you done with my clothes?'

CHAPTER NINE

KHALED dismissed the women with a flick of his hand.

'You don't like your new garments?'

'These things aren't mine. What have you done with the clothes I packed?'

'I promised you a gift—the garments made by Hebra's best seamstresses. Do you agree they are quite beautiful?'

'I want my clothes.'

'Your clothes were not appropriate for the desert. This isn't Milan or Sydney or even Hebra. Aren't you going to try these on? See how well they fit? See how well they become you?'

'Why the hell should I?'

'Because,' he said, his dark eyes shiny with victory, 'you have no choice. You have nothing else to wear.'

'Then I'll wear what I've already got on.'

His nostrils flared. 'It is entirely up to you if you wish to offend our hosts. For while we value the camel for transport, it is not a beast we would choose to eat with.'

She spun away from him, determined that he wouldn't see that she knew he was right. From the moment they'd arrived at the encampment she'd looked forward to the prospect of washing off the baggage of a long, dusty trip and changing into clean clothes. But her idea of clean clothes had more to do with a linen skirt and fresh blouse than the silky nothingness of the fabrics now contained in her suitcase.

'You need not be concerned,' he said, almost as if he could read her thoughts. 'It makes no difference what you had planned to wear as no one would see it anyway. The women will provide you with an *abaya* and *hijab*, a cloak and scarf to cover your garments and head, and a *burka* to hide your face, as is the custom here in the tribes. All anyone will see of you is your eyes. So you see, you really have nothing to get upset about.'

'In that case,' she said at last, 'it would appear that I don't have much of a choice.'

'No,' he said, 'you don't.'

And then he was gone, leaving her and her resentment simmering in his wake.

All night long the blue eyes had captivated him. All night he'd wished for a halt to the seemingly endless cups of coffee, the conversation that lingered interminably, when all he wanted to do was be alone with her.

Even covered from head to toe she stood out. There was simply no way Sapphire would blend in by dressing her in the local garb. There was no way she would not be noticed.

All anyone could see was her blue eyes, clear and warm, shining from behind her cotton *burka*. Yet he could see the way they lit up when she laughed, the way they creased at the corners with delight, the way they reacted when others told their tales of desert wanderings or their children, the way they would fill with compassion when the story was sad.

Most of all he liked the way they stilled when his gaze locked on hers, smoke suddenly swirling in their depths before they dropped or turned away.

All he could see was her blue eyes and even they were enough to hold him transfixed. Yet the promise, too, of what was under the dark *abaya* intervened in his thoughts. He wanted to strip away the cloak, to find the woman under the dull garb, to explore her feminine shape and hidden curves.

And now, when their hosts had finally called an end to the evening, now he finally had his chance.

She clutched the sides of the *abaya*, avoiding looking at him directly as Khaled walked her to her tent, the soft maa-ing of the goats carrying gently across the crisp night air. It was cooler now although feeling warm didn't seem to be a problem for her. Not given the way Khaled had made her feel through dinner.

Tonight he looked more like a sheikh than ever. For the first time he had put aside the western garb she was used to seeing him in and that was so much a part of business in modern Hebra and instead he wore the traditional robes of the region. In the fine white shirt, the traditional headdress with its double cord of woven goat-hair and sheep's wool, and the long black robes edged with gold braid, Khaled looked larger than life, a real desert king.

She'd seen the way he'd watched her tonight, had

felt his eyes on her, and on those times she'd been unable to resist looking his way she'd been held by the authority of his features, the sheer power of his eyes, the potent message they contained.

He wanted her.

Sure, she'd known it before, she'd felt his need on his lips and in his kiss, but never had it taken on the significance it had now, the way it rocked her as they made their way almost silently across the pebble-strewn sands to her tent. He knew she was leaving yet still he wanted her.

Under her long robe a multitude of sensations beset her. Silk slid across her skin at every move, the metal belt shimmying softly over her hips, and tiny bells jangled softly on her ankles. She felt ultra-feminine, exquisitely sensual and sexy in a way she never had before.

Was it the garments that lay hidden under the *abaya* or was it the way Khaled had looked at her through dinner, as though he was already slowly peeling off her clothes, that made her flesh tingle and gave her such a rush of moist heat?

It didn't matter. What suddenly did was the realisation that she could no longer deny.

She wanted him too.

It made no sense. She was leaving soon. Returning to her fashion-industry life in Milan and leaving the desert far behind her. She was getting what she really wanted, wasn't she? Escape and freedom. Whereas Khaled meant the exact opposite. Khaled would keep her here forever. Even though his crazy marriage plans had been aborted, she knew he would possess her if she let him. How then could she even imagine that she wanted any part of him?

But imagination didn't come into it. What she wanted was real.

They reached her tent, and he followed her through the opening, the heaviness of her need threatening to swamp her, to drown all rational thought. Suddenly she didn't want to say goodnight. Suddenly she wanted to prolong this moment, this time out here, in the soft lamplight of a lush Bedouin tent.

He placed one hand on her shoulder, angling her towards him. 'You have the most expressive eyes, did you know?' He lifted the other hand to her mask, tracing her cheek through the fabric. 'You didn't mind wearing this? It must seem strange to you.'

'It's all right,' she said. Her voice sounded clouded and thick. 'It's the custom here. I don't mind.'

'Well, you have no need of it now,' he said, his hand reaching behind to release the tie that held it in place. It dropped to the floor at the same time he removed her scarf. Automatically she reached up a hand to smooth back her hair, suddenly nervous, expectant.

'Your cloak too,' he said, his voice heavy with need. 'If you wish.'

She hesitated fractionally. It was only an outer robe, but by taking it off, what was she saying to him? The silken garments that she wore beneath hardly constituted a barrier between them. But then, the way her body was humming, her need accelerating, maybe it was time the barriers came down.

Her fingers fumbled their way to the closures that ran from her neck to her waist, undoing them in turn. Only when she had finished, her hands unsure of where to go next, did he put his hands to her shoulders, parting the robe and peeling it down her arms, finally letting go and allowing its weight to drag it to the floor, exposing her to his gaze.

She held her breath.

Breath hissed through his teeth. After the severity and relative shapelessness of the *abaya*, he had expected that her feminine shape in the garments his seamstresses had prepared would please him. But his thoughts and preconceptions had in no way prepared him for this.

She was a goddess.

The blue skirt hugged her low down on her hips, the golden threads of the fabric winking in the lamplight with every tiny movement, the shadow of her long legs an enticing promise beneath. More gold bound her breasts, concealing even as it accentuated her womanly curves, leaving bare the exquisite skinscape of her midriff.

She might not have been happy about having her clothes swapped but right now she didn't look as if she held it against him. He'd wanted to strip away all the shackles of her previous life, to let her absorb and enjoy the full experience of the desert without the barrier of western clothes to hide behind.

And, if he was honest, there was more than a modicum of self-interest involved. He'd longed to see her out of her usual attire, her well-designed yet far too tailored attire.

Now he had, he was sure he would never have his fill. She was a feast for the eyes. His body reacted in the only way possible. Inside him the hunger cranked up a notch, the need to possess her all-consuming.

When he didn't move she lifted her eyes fractionally, afraid of what she might see in his. She wasn't disappointed. Hot appreciation, vivid and intent, blazed out of their dark depths, his chin set rigid as if he was holding himself tightly under control.

Sparks ignited inside her, sparks that fired messages to nerve endings that tingled and buzzed. Flesh responded, exposed skin goose-pimpled, breasts peaked and firmed.

Then his mouth slanted over hers and the feelings were magnified, intensified, as his need fed into hers. She tasted coffee, the desert and passion, the power that was Khaled alive in his kiss as his lips moved over hers, as his tongue explored her depths.

His arms curled around her, pulling her in close to him, his hands warm on the dip of her spine, the flare of her hips, the curve of her breast.

Pressure mounted inside her, pressure that turned the dull ache between her thighs into more like a pulsing imperative. Her hands tangled through the metres of cloth that made up his robes, wanting to feel not his clothes, but his body, firm and hard, next to hers.

And close up she could feel his strength, feel the

power of his need as she pressed herself against the firm ridge of his erection.

His head drew back on a shudder as his arms loosened and she looked up, confused, missing his heat already.

'Sapphire,' he said, his voice a bare rasp, his breath fast and choppy.

And instantly she was reminded of the times before, when he'd kissed her and pulled away, leaving her reeling and hungry for more and resentful of his control, and she knew that no way was he doing that to her again. She couldn't bear it.

This was most likely her last night in Jebbai. Her last night with Khaled. Her last chance to satisfy this reckless desire that flared whenever he was near.

Soon she'd be back in Milan, alone in her apartment, no Paolo to console her, nothing to ease her regret for missing out on what she could have had.

So this time would be different. This time he wasn't leaving her cold. This time he could damn well finish what he'd started.

She anchored her arms around his neck and pulled herself tight up against him. 'Khaled,' she whispered, her lips close to his ear, pressing tiny kisses along his throat, nipping his skin with her teeth and pressing her breasts into his chest. 'Make love to me.'

CHAPTER TEN

HE SEEMED to hesitate a moment, almost as if he didn't believe what he'd heard. But only for a moment.

Then his eyes sparked white heat and he uttered something low and guttural, the words indiscernible to her but his intentions clear. He collected her in his arms and lifted her out of the circle of her discarded robe, breaching the distance to the bed in three long strides.

He laid her down, amongst the soft covers and tasselled cushions, and knelt beside her, his chest rising powerfully, drinking her in with his eyes.

'Magnificent,' he said, his words curling into her senses, feeding the fires inside, as he shrugged off his cloak and tore his headdress away. Then he dipped his head and reefed his long shirt over his back and shoulders, balling it in his hands before flinging it across the tent.

She didn't see where it landed. Her eyes were on him, on the golden skin of his chest, glowing warmly in the soft lamplight.

His shoulders were broad, his muscles well defined, his skin satin-smooth. She reached out a hand to touch him, spreading her fingers, relishing the feel of his firm abdomen, anticipating what lay below the loose white trousers that were his only remaining garment. Her fingers dropped to the waistband, slipping inside.

Breath hissed through his teeth as one hand whipped out, snaring hers. And what she saw in his eyes—desire, raw and urgent, naked and demanding—edged up her own hunger. He pushed her arm down onto the bed, stretching himself out lengthwise alongside, his leg situating itself between hers, dipping his mouth to hers once more.

Then she was lost in his kisses, lost in his touch and in the heat he generated inside her. There were too many sensations, too much to assimilate, such that all she could think of while he explored her body, setting fires wherever he touched, was that he felt so good.

He felt so right.

His hand cupped her breast, his kisses trailing down her neck until his mouth too was there. Even through the fabric his hot breath hit home, her nipple budding tight between his teeth.

He moved suddenly and reached around her. Then her top was slipping down her arms and cool air met her exposed breasts. Cool air and his hot gaze. He made a sound like a growl, low and deep, before his head dipped first to one nipple, gently lapping, suckling, rolling the nipple, before turning his attentions to the other.

It was torture. Her head rocked from one side to the other. *Exquisite torture*—but still it wasn't enough.

His hand ran down the length of her leg, floating

down the silken layers of her skirt, and then up again, this time shucking the filmy fabric out of his path. Nerve endings screamed along the length of her body, sending off needle-like charges that speared direct to just one place.

She felt liquid inside, molten, as his hand caressed her thigh—close, so close—and then he touched her there and her back arched as light like a flash bulb went off in the recesses of her closed eyes. His touch was gentle, sensual, erotic and she felt herself responding to him, opening, yielding.

Yet still it wasn't enough.

'Khaled,' she pleaded, her hands tangled in his hair, wanting an end to the waiting, an end to the anticipation. 'Please.'

He lifted his head from her breast and looked up at her, his dark eyes smouldering, so heavy with intent that it rocked her.

'Nothing could give me greater pleasure,' he said, raising himself up to his knees and tugging down his cotton trousers. Her eyes followed the motion, held captive by the sheer beauty of his form, unable to tear her eyes away from his sculpted torso, his flat stomach and down further, where the cotton fabric provided no restraint...

And then he was free and anticipation gave way to apprehension.

He was magnificent.

She swallowed, suddenly less sure of herself. But he allowed her no chance to reconsider as he leant over, his mouth meshing with hers, telling her in no uncertain terms that whatever her concerns, he had none.

She lost herself again in his mouth as he pressed himself close to her and in a few deft moves she realised that her skirt had been efficiently despatched and her legs laid bare. Then his fingers slid under the lace of her thong until even that was slipped away and awareness and expectation washed over her like a tide.

Thigh against thigh. Breast against breast. Skin against skin. They rolled together on the bed, a tangle of limbs, and with the hot promise of more. And with the last barriers gone, there was nothing to stop them. She was glad. She wanted him inside her, so he could be part of her, so they could be part of each other.

He rolled away suddenly and she felt cold, exposed, until she realised what he was doing. But by then he was back and her mind processed his sensible actions with gratitude and appreciation.

And it meant, oh, it meant that soon there would be an end to this endless aching need.

He held her face in his hands, kissing her tenderly on her eyes, her cheeks, her chin as the seconds spun out in the suspense of waiting for the inevitable.

Inevitable.

Ever since Khaled had entered Bacelli's salon, this moment had been unavoidable. Even from that first moment the attraction between them had been apparent. And ever since then it had been building, smouldering away, gathering force in spite of all that had happened to force them apart, despite all she had done to protect herself.

This moment was her destiny, her fate.

He took her mouth again as he raised himself up onto his elbows, positioning himself above her. His eyelids were heavy, his brow glossed satin with sweat.

She felt his weight, settling at her entrance, testing, probing, and instinctively she lifted her hips to welcome him with her own slick need, wanting him closer still, needing the completion, needing to have him deep inside.

And then he was. He plunged full length, driving his hips into hers, throwing back his head as if in triumph as his back arched over her.

Time stood still. She was unable to breathe, unable to think, unaware of anything beyond the exquisite sensation of him stretching her, of him filling her completely.

And then he moved inside her and a new wave of nerve endings came into play. Slowly he withdrew, only to fill her again and then again, and with each thrust the sensations grew, the pleasure mounted, wave upon wave of sheer ecstasy, building, always building.

She could feel his tension in his corded arms, she could sense his own battle for control, she could feel her mounting need for release mirrored in his own as the waves rolled in, the rhythm quickening and threatening to carry her away.

And then he took her there himself, with one final

thrust that sent them both spiralling, shattering out of control, sending a tidal wave of sensation crashing over them, violent and primal, until it left them sweat-slickened and panting, their bodies spent, like so much driftwood left on the shore.

It was enough. She came to slowly, her pulse steadying, her body humming, dimly aware that, while it was still late at night, this was a brand-new day; and that, although she was still Sapphy Clemenger, on another level she was a stranger, even to herself.

She looked at him, settled into her shoulder, his eyes closed, his steadying breaths warm on her breast, his beautiful body majestic even in repose.

He'd changed her.

Never before had she experienced such need, such desire, and never in her wildest dreams had she imagined that lovemaking could be so mind-blowingly spectacular. Not that it had been bad before, just that in hindsight it seemed as though making love had been on another level, almost as if some vital ingredient had been missing.

If this night gave her nothing more, she would indeed have some warm memories to keep her company during her lonely nights back in her apartment in Milan.

Milan. She sucked in a breath. She'd be back there in less than two days, assuming the airport reopened as planned. And for all her desperation to escape from Khaled and return to Italy, the city itself had lost some of its appeal. Somehow she couldn't see herself slotting straight back into work. Even involved in the crazy, fast-paced fashion industry, it was going to seem strangely dull after her visit to Jebbai with its enigmatic ruler.

Maybe first she should take some leave, go home to Australia and visit her sisters and Pearl and check up on her baby niece. She was owed some time and it wasn't as if she couldn't start sketching up designs for the next collection while she was travelling. She'd talk to Gianfranco as soon as she was back in Milan.

His eyes blinked open and she realised she'd been staring at his face the whole time. He smiled and reached out a hand, stroking it down the side of her face and brushing away the loose strands of hair.

'You look...deep in thought,' he said, his voice rich and low enough to make her toes curl all over again.

She flicked her gaze away. He didn't need to know she was having second thoughts about returning straight to Milan. It wasn't as if it had anything to do with him. 'I was just—thinking about my family.'

He rolled closer, pressing his lips to her neck. 'You don't talk about them much, apart from when you went camel riding with your sisters. Tell me about them.'

She tried to ignore the feeling of his mouth leaving tiny kisses along her collar-bone, although the sensation was strangely soothing while at the same time it seemed highly erotic.

'I haven't seen them for far too long.'

'You're not close?'

'We used to be closer.'

'What changed things?'

She drew in a deep breath and rolled over, away from the distraction of his mouth, to somewhere bland she could direct her words, like the pillow in front of her. 'Oh, it was nothing bad. My mother came back…'

He said nothing for a few seconds. Then, 'I don't understand.'

She turned her face back to him. 'We thought she'd died when Ruby and I were four. It turns out she'd been living in exile at that time—banished by our father.'

'How did you find her?'

'Opal's husband, Domenic, tracked her down to where she was living in England. He took her back to Sydney. She lives there now, in the family hotel that Opal runs. Dad died a couple of years before. He was always busy when we were young and it was usually just the three of us girls growing up with the nanny of the day. But Opal was our big sister. She looked after us better than anyone.'

'You don't like your mother?'

'Oh, no. Don't get me wrong. Pearl is lovely. It's just hard to come to grips with the idea that I have a mother at all. For years we thought she was dead. And now she's there and it's just not the same any more. Opal has a baby girl, Ellie, who's toddling now, and Pearl and Opal are very close. And Ruby works in Broome and is just so very far away.'

He curled his arm around her shoulder, gathering her in close to his chest, stroking her hair.

'I see,' he said, softly kissing the top of her head. 'You've gained a mother, yet it feels like you've lost your sisters.'

She blinked against the warmth of his skin, surprised that he understood so much. 'Yes. That's exactly how it feels—except it's still not like I can even accept her as my mother. She was gone too long. And now I don't even know my sisters. Does that make sense?'

'It makes sense. It is never easy to lose the ones we love,' he said, his words trailing off, his hand stilling in her hair.

She almost groaned out loud when she realised. Here she was feeling sorry for herself and Khaled had known *real* loss. Both his parents, killed in tragic circumstances. He'd probably give anything for his mother to be alive. And yet she was acting as if her mother's return had ruined her life.

'Khaled,' she said, lifting herself up so she could see him, 'I'm so sorry. I didn't think.'

Even in the dim lights, his eyes shone bright and glossy, their dark depths granite-hard, his chin set rigid as he stared unseeing at the ceiling. Then he looked at her and something inside them slowly peeled away.

It wasn't her fault. He looked into her concerned blue eyes, his hand resuming its stroking motion of her hair, and knew that, despite her associations, it had nothing to do with her. It was Paolo who was to blame, it was Paolo who would pay. Already he would be suffering, his imagination no doubt conjuring up all sorts of despicable ways in which Khaled would be taking advantage of his one-time fiancée.

He allowed himself a smile. It was almost funny. How much worse was Paolo going to feel when he discovered the truth—that he hadn't needed to take her by force? That it was Sapphy who'd asked him to make love to her. How much worse would he feel when he discovered that she was not a prisoner—but that she had decided to stay in Jebbai, as she surely now would, of her own accord?

No doubt the irony would not be lost on Paolo.

But then, in another way, it didn't matter what Paolo thought. For right now he didn't matter. Sapphire was here with him now, it was his scent she would smell on her, it was his body holding hers.

'It must have been a dreadful time for you,' she said, the breath behind her words falling like warm caresses on his skin. He sucked in a breath. She was much too special for anyone else. He could listen to her gentle words all day. He could watch the way her rounded breasts, her nipples peaked and taut, brushed against his chest forever. That was, unless he was doing something much more satisfying.

'It wasn't a good time,' he agreed, feeling his need rising with the sudden urge to do something much more satisfying. He flipped her over onto her back again, enjoying her whoop of surprise and the way her eyes widened first with shock and then with anticipation.

'But right now is a whole lot better.'

He made love to her then, slowly, deliberately, taking his time, exploring her body and sharing the initiative with her when she chose to explore his. And this time was even better than the first, more tender and yet more passionate, more exploratory and yet more focused. She was everything he thought she'd be as a lover and more.

And only when finally they'd both tumbled over the edge of reason again, only when he'd seen the blue facets of her eyes spark and flare into a fire that consumed them both, did he follow her into sleep.

The goats woke her—with their early-morning bleating for attention and the soft jangle of their bells as the first hint of dawn light permeated the tent's walls, reminding her of where she was. But once awake, it was the heated body of the man who slept alongside her amongst the tangled sheets and the musky scent of their lovemaking that proved the distraction.

She propped herself up on one elbow and drank him in. He lay on his stomach, his head to one side, his arms high on the pillow. The remnants of one sheet was slanted across his thighs, so that his well-defined back was exposed from his broad shoulders to his tight waist and even tighter mounds of his rump below. She sucked in a breath.

How could he do that? How could he look so damned sexy when he was still asleep?

Memories of the night's activities came flooding back in a rush of heat, bringing a smile to her mouth. Hot memories. Her flesh quivered at the images playing over in her mind, at the same time rarely used muscles ached their protests, bringing to mind more of Khaled's seductive night moves.

Her muscles would recover. In a day or two they'd forget and be back to normal. Not so her. Last night would be a night she'd remember for a long time to come. And after last night, *normal* was going to seem exceedingly dull.

What would it be like to have Khaled in her bed every night? To share passion and desire with him, night after night and then to wake up with him alongside her every morning? What would that be like?

She'd thrown away the chance to find out.

Realisation hit her like a cold shower. If she'd agreed to become his wife she could expect that—Khaled in her bed, every night, every morning, *every way*.

She'd had the chance and she'd thrown it away when she'd thrown his crazy marriage plans back in his face.

She sighed and eased herself back down onto her pillow, staring up at the tent's ceiling. She'd done the right thing. It had been a crazy marriage plan—he'd been way out of line, scheming and conspiring to make her his wife in his own version of an arranged marriage—and she'd had no choice but to refuse. Any sane person would.

Why had he ever imagined she'd go along with it? It didn't make sense and the more she came to learn about Khaled, the less sense it made. He was a strong leader, respected and loved by his people. She'd seen this with her own eyes, he was both fair and good in dealings with them. He was no petty despot.

And with his good looks he could have his pick of women to be his bride. So what could possibly have driven him to choose her?

None of it made sense. So she *had* done the right thing. She knew it. Despite the sex. Even if she couldn't imagine ever tiring of feeling the way he'd made her feel last night, sex just wasn't enough. For since when did compatibility in bed constitute a sound basis for marriage anyway? It wasn't as if they were in love with each other after all.

Oh, she'd miss him when she returned to Milan, that was true. She'd miss catching his hooded gaze upon her when she looked up, and his brooding magnetism setting her nerve endings alight. She'd even miss the verbal sparring between them and the endless mounting tension.

And there were times she even liked him. Though that was hardly the same thing as love.

Hardly the same thing at all…

On impulse she leaned over to him, his face still turned into the pillow. Holding back her hair with one hand, she dipped her head and kissed him.

His eyelids batted open and he smiled, uttering a low growl as one arm came down and circled around her.

'Thank you,' he said.

She smiled back. 'I think it was my pleasure.'

'It was our pleasure,' he purred, nuzzling her ear. 'You are so beautiful. I cannot understand why any man would be crazy enough to choose another over you.'

She went rigid. Paolo hadn't even entered into her thoughts and right now was hardly the time to bring him up. Not that she felt guilty. It wasn't as if they were still involved in a relationship and she'd betrayed him by sleeping with Khaled, not given her last phone call to him that had signalled the end of their relationship.

But still she didn't want to think of Paolo when she was in another man's arms. The shock of Paolo's deception was still too raw, too painful. She didn't want to be reminded of it now. She didn't need to be reminded of it now.

Tell me you enjoyed making love to me, she wished; *tell me it was worth it. But don't remind me that someone else thought I wasn't.*

He cursed under his breath. What was he thinking? He had done what he had set out to do. He had made her want him and then he had made her his own. But his victory over Paolo was for his satisfaction—he should never have mentioned his name. Not when she was probably still mourning the loss of their relationship.

He pushed himself up, scooping her into his arms, kissing her averted cheek. 'I'm sorry,' he said. 'That was a stupid thing to say. But there is one thing I'll never be sorry about.'

A blink of her eyelids, the soft parting of her lips on a sigh, was her only response.

'I could never be sorry that you are here, in my arms and in my bed. I will never be sorry for that, for as long as I live. I don't think I could ever have enough of you.'

She took a deep breath, her chest rising in a way that could not escape his attention. He couldn't resist. He dropped his mouth over the closest nipple, rolling it languidly between his lips with his tongue, to be rewarded almost immediately with her gasp of pleasure as the nipple peaked in his mouth. Then he lifted his head fractionally, blowing softly on to the tip, fascinated to watch it pebble and firm.

She trembled in his arms as he drew closer to the other nipple. 'Prove it,' she invited.

The capital was bustling with afternoon crowds and swirling traffic by the time they neared the palace. She sat quietly in the Range Rover, the return trip having gone all too quickly for her liking, and she cursed the invention of the internal combustion engine that saw her sitting in a luxurious leather bucket seat, so far from Khaled's reach, when a century ago she might have been sharing his saddle the entire journey.

The journey on camels from the encampment back to the vehicles had been the best. Almost every part of her felt tender, her aches a welcome reminder of their night of passion, and she'd let herself relax into his body, had even found ways she could inveigle herself closer still, pressing her face to his chest, relishing the scent of man, rich and raw, as it fed into her senses.

Even after a night and morning of passion she was still burning for him. She couldn't help it. Back home in Australia his touch would come with a government health warning—it was dangerously addictive. And after a night spent revelling in his touch, and a ride together through the desert dunes on a loping camel on their way to meet the cars, the more addicted she'd become.

It was going to be more of a wrench to leave than she could ever have imagined. Surprisingly more of a wrench, given yesterday she'd been demanding to be taken to the airport so she could leave the country immediately. She'd been so sure then, so absolutely driven to escape the first chance she had.

Why now, then, was she in two minds about leaving? Why, barely more than twenty-four hours later, was the thought of heading for the airport so much less compelling?

What had changed, other than they'd made love, out there in a tent amongst the desert sands?

Unless this wasn't just about sex? Unless…

No way!

There was no way. Between them there was just sex. It was just a physical thing. There could only ever be just sex.

So why did the thought of leaving Jebbai, of leaving Khaled, seem to tear a hole right through her? Seem to gut her completely? Why did the closer she got to saying goodbye for ever make her less and less comfortable? It couldn't only be put down to the best sex she'd ever had, surely.

'What's wrong?' said Khaled from the driver's seat.

'What do you mean, what's wrong?' she asked, suddenly aware that she'd been shaking her head from side to side.

'You don't look happy. Would you have liked to stay longer in the desert?'

Heat suffused his words and swirled the depths of his eyes and she saw the pictures he must be thinking, she could feel his touch on her skin. 'Oh, no,' she lied, her voice shaky as the bottom fell out of her world with the power of her discovery. 'It was an interesting trip, but it's such a relief to be back.'

Her voice choked up on the last word but still she managed to dredge up a bright smile from somewhere. His eyes hardened, taking on a granite sheen as he measured her words, and she wished he'd look back at the road before they veered off it.

Finally he looked to the front again and she felt

her smile crack and slide away. How much longer could she keep this up now that it had hit her? Now that one sight of the reflection in his dark eyes had confirmed what she'd feared was true.

Damn it all. She'd known this would happen if she'd stayed. She'd known she was in danger of falling more and more under Khaled's magnetic spell if she didn't get away.

And it had happened. The worst thing possible had happened.

This wasn't about sex.

This had never been about sex.

She'd fallen in love with Khaled.

CHAPTER ELEVEN

SHE had to get away. Now more than ever. No longer could she trust what she felt and she couldn't even be sure she was thinking straight any more. She'd lost control of her life and she needed time away to try and get it back.

Away from Khaled's influence and powerful spell she could be more objective and clear-headed. A break spent with her family in Australia would give her the distance she needed to get herself back together. She had bridges to rebuild there as it was, with her mother and sisters, before she could consider moving on. Gianfranco had to allow her the leave. He just had to.

But the first step to doing any of that was to get away from Jebbai.

She was quiet as Khaled pulled the vehicle to a halt outside the palace, reluctant to speak until he had shaken off the servants and carried her bag back to her room himself.

'There,' he said, opening the door to her study and putting down her bag. 'Back safe and sound. Didn't I say so?' He looked around the apartment. 'Where's Azizah? She should be here.'

'Maybe she wasn't expecting us back so soon,' she

said, wishing he would go, wishing he would stay, wishing it was all over.

She glanced down at her watch, mentally adding a six-hour journey to the early-afternoon time and thinking it might still be possible to arrange a flight back to Milan today if the security alert was over. Compared to that it really wasn't important where Azizah was in the scheme of things. It wasn't as if she needed anyone to help her pack. And it wasn't as if she could put off the question that had been plaguing her thoughts.

'Is there any news of the airport reopening?'

He stiffened, the long, fluid lines of his body pulling up tall and taut.

'Is that a passing enquiry, or do you have a more specific interest?'

She swallowed back her first response. How could he pretend not to know why she cared?

'Why do you ask? Will it make your answer any different?'

'I want to know. Why do you care whether the airport is open or closed?'

'Because you said you'd give me a lift, remember? You promised to take me to the airport and put me on a plane for Milan, just as soon as it reopened.'

Silence met her words, a fat, incredulous bubble of silence.

Then it burst. 'You're still planning on leaving?' Disbelief turned his words into an accusation.

'Of course I am. I told you I wanted to leave. You

told me you'd take me to the airport yourself. You promised.'

He took two strides towards her. 'But that was before…' His words trailed off.

'Before what?' she demanded. 'Before last night? You think that what happened last night changes anything?'

His eyebrows lifted. 'Doesn't it?'

'We had sex, Khaled,' she said. 'People do it all the time and then they walk away. End of story.' She shrugged. 'It changes nothing.' She turned her head, before he could see the lie in her eyes. Before he could see how her own words tore at her heart. She couldn't let him see what it meant to her, not when she was so vulnerable and afraid and desperate to escape.

'Sex?' The word erupted from him like a cannonball as her forearm was grabbed in his iron-like grasp, pulling her back around to face him. 'Is that what we had? And all the time I thought we were making love.'

'Call it whatever you like,' she said more shakily than she wished. 'You promised to take me to the airport.' She looked up at him, her eyes pleading for him to understand. 'And I'm holding you to it.'

He let go of her arm, wheeling away, raking one clawed hand through his hair.

'I don't want you to go.'

She squeezed her eyes shut, clamping back on the stinging dampness behind her lids. 'We've been through this.'

He spun around to face her. 'No, we haven't.'

'Khaled—'

'No!' he shouted. 'When I made that promise I thought I could let you walk out of my life if you wanted to. I really believed it. But I thought it wouldn't come to that—I thought I would change your mind about leaving—that you would decide to stay here in Jebbai with me.'

She laughed, the sound coming brittle and harsh. 'You thought one night with you would change my mind? You really must fancy yourself as some sort of Arab stud.'

His eyes flashed with danger, his jaw rigid as concrete, and she stepped back, fearing she had gone too far.

'Listen to me,' he hissed, his teeth clenched, his eyes rapier sharp. 'No one has ever felt so right in my bed, such liquid fire in my arms. That perfect moment when we two became one—you could not help but feel that. I know you felt it too. You can't deny it.'

There was no oxygen left in the room, otherwise why was it so difficult to breathe? So difficult to think?

'Khaled, I…'

'I don't want you to go, Sapphire. Even if last night changed nothing for you, it changed the world for me. After last night I know I could never live without you. The last thing I want to do in the world is to take you to the airport never to see you again. I can't lose you now. I want you to stay here and become my wife.'

'No,' she protested, vehemently shaking her head as she tried to dislodge his hand on her arm. 'That's crazy. That's exactly why you brought me here in the first place! Why should this time be any different?'

His free hand cupped her cheek. She flinched, trying to pull away, but his hand remained, and against her own better judgement she found herself nestling into the warm strength of his palm. His face hovered just inches from her own, his eyes suddenly more tender than she'd ever seen.

'Something happened to me last night, while I was out there in that desert tent with you. I discovered something momentous that I should have realised long, long ago.'

She was afraid to blink, afraid to breathe, afraid the sound of her pumping heart would drown out his words.

'Zafeerah…' The way he said her name fed into her soul, he might have been worshipping her. 'I'm not good at showing these things, but can't you feel it? I love you.'

Her pulse quickened, thumping in her chest as his words hit home. *He loved her?* How could it be possible, after all that had happened?

'You don't believe me,' he said, 'but you must. I think I loved you from the very first time I saw you in the salon. I wanted you back then but it has taken me all this time to see the truth of what was staring me in the face all along.

'I love you. And that's why I cannot bear the

thought of your leaving. I want you to stay and be by my side forever. I am asking you to become my wife.'

His mouth slanted over hers and she felt his lips, heated, filled with promise and expectation, moving over hers.

She felt her resolve to leave wavering, losing balance in a world she was less and less sure of. So much was changing and all too fast. Her heart sang with his revelation yet at the same time her mind reeled.

She couldn't think straight before he'd made his announcement. How could she possibly think straight now?

He lifted his head, his hands taking hers in his. 'Will you stay then? Will you stay, and become my wife?'

She could tell him now that she felt the same way, that she too had fallen and fallen hard, but there was still too much to think about, too much history to get over, too many things to forgive.

She started to shake her head. 'I don't know.'

'Please,' he implored. 'Please think about it.'

He was so different now. This was a man used to getting what he wanted. All he had to do was click his fingers and people came running. Yet he was asking her now, pleading with her to reconsider.

She could see what this was costing him, could see the pain and uncertainty in his features. It was a different side of Khaled—a much more vulnerable and human side than she'd seen before.

Maybe he was speaking the truth. Maybe he did

love her. But how could she be sure? After all the half-truths and secrets, it was all too much to process.

'Think about it,' he repeated, sensing her own bewilderment. 'I'll leave you now. Take your time; call me on the intercom when you've made up your mind. The airport has reopened. I'll have my jet put on standby. If you still want to leave, you can leave immediately. On the other hand, if you decide to stay…'

His words trailed off and she nodded. 'Thank you,' she said, thinking how inadequate that sounded after such a conversation.

He smiled and pressed his lips to her forehead. Then he turned and left, pulling the door softly closed behind him.

It seemed like years since she'd been in the workshop, yet it was really only yesterday. Azizah had still not shown up, so there was no opportunity to distract herself with small talk and minor housekeeping issues. Instead, as she prowled amongst the worktables bearing machines all now empty and silent, her thoughts kept churning, going over and over trying to digest the impact of Khaled's surprise declaration, trying to fit all the pieces together.

He loved her.

She loved him.

He wanted to marry her.

She wanted to get away.

Or did she?

Her reason for leaving was to keep herself safe, to protect herself from Khaled's influence. But what would she be saving when she'd already lost her heart? What more was there to risk when her body wanted nothing more than to be pressed close next to his?

Would it be so wrong to stay and marry him? To have him as her partner, in bed and out of it for her entire life? Was that not preferable to turning her back on their love and living without him, alone somewhere and full of regrets for what might have been?

It was still so difficult to think, but maybe this was how it was supposed to be—a decision that should be made not with the head, but with the heart. What could she lose by doing what her heart knew instinctively was right?

In the corner of the room the wedding dress that had brought her to Jebbai still hung on the mannequin, its brilliant beaded and jewelled bodice gleaming even through the clear protective dust jacket. The sight of it brought a smile to her face, even in the midst of her inner turmoil.

If she'd achieved anything in Jebbai, it was this gown. It was beautiful, the most beautiful she'd ever seen and most certainly the most beautiful she'd ever made. The design was exquisite and, thanks to the skill and dedication of her assistants, the workmanship second to none.

And it could still be hers...

Sensation shimmied down her spine at the possibility and she bit down hard on her bottom lip as carefully she peeled back the protective layer, revealing the full splendour of the dress.

It had been made to her measurements, certainly, but with not one fitting. And the real test of any garment was not how it looked hanging up, but how it looked on the person it had been designed for. How well had they transformed a bare set of measurements and metres of fabric into a gown for a real woman? There was still the possibility she might leave Jebbai and never know.

There was only one way to find out.

The dress slipped sensually over her skin, cool and satin smooth after she'd stripped off the cotton shirt and chinos she'd worn for the return journey. There was weight in the gown, much more than was apparent at first glance, but the weight felt balanced in the long skirt that flared out from her hips. She did up as many of the pearl fastenings at her back as she could, thinking it would be so much easier with someone to help her but at the same time thankful there was no one to witness her folly.

There was a full-length mirror in her walk-in wardrobe. And heeled shoes. She hitched up the heavy train and headed for her bedroom, feeling heady with both exhilaration and recklessness.

She saw it propped up against her telephone as soon as she walked through the door into the office. She'd completely missed the envelope when she'd first arrived, too preoccupied talking to Khaled, her back to the desk. But from the door the angle was perfect and she could not miss it.

Who was writing to her here? Unless it was Gianfranco, although it was more usual for him just to send a fax. Curious, she picked up the envelope on the way through to her dressing room. The outside gave nothing away, the typewritten address bland and uninformative. Likewise the absence of a return address.

She shrugged and flipped the envelope down onto her bed as she passed. The letter could wait. First to the shoes. She searched her wardrobe, where her gear had been returned since her aborted attempt to leave yesterday, and hauled out the highest pair of heels she'd brought. They were brightly coloured sandals, hardly a good match, but they'd give her the extra height she needed to get the best impression of the fall of the dress.

She slipped them on, smoothing down the material, impatient now for her first glance in the mirror. She twisted her hair into a knot on the top of her head, took a deep breath and stepped in front of the mirror.

Oh, wow!

It looked—sensational.

The dress fitted her like a second skin, moulding itself perfectly to every dip, every curve, while its exquisite lines spoke elegance. She looked instantly taller, more regal. But if it looked fantastic, it felt even better. Even in this hurried try-on state, without make-up or her hair done properly, the dress felt superb.

More than that, it felt right.

Her teeth found her lip again. It did feel right. Just as making love with Khaled in the desert tent had felt so perfect, as if they were destined to be forever.

Maybe this wedding was preordained too. Maybe it was written in the stars and all she'd had to do was to say yes. Had Khaled felt that all along? Was that why he'd concocted his plan to lure her to his desert kingdom and win her heart?

A bubble of laughter welled up inside her and in her excitement she couldn't hold it back. Neither that nor the mistiness that suddenly filled her eyes. Her hands flew to her mouth as the sheer craziness of what was happening hit home.

Yesterday she hadn't thought it possible. There'd been no way she would have contemplated marriage, despite the attraction growing between them. But yesterday she'd known nothing of his love for her and she'd had even less idea of her own love for him.

She turned this way and that in the mirror, allowing herself one final appraisal. She'd never thought herself a fairy-tale princess, but she sure felt like it in this dress. The only things missing were her veil, a bouquet of fresh flowers—and a handsome prince.

Although she had one of those just waiting for her call.

All she had to do was pick up the phone.

Then he would be here. And she wouldn't even have to tell him—one look at her in the wedding dress and he would have his answer.

She picked up the phone next to her bed and dialled.

CHAPTER TWELVE

Ten minutes, Saleem had told her, Khaled would be along then. Meanwhile he'd seemed more interested in whether or not Azizah had shown up yet.

Deflated and suddenly filled with nervous tension, she paced the room, wanting something to stop her thinking. Now she'd made up her mind, the last thing she wanted was more time to think.

Her eyes fell upon the letter where she'd discarded it on the bed and gratefully she scooped it up. It would serve as a distraction, at least for a minute or two. She tore it open and unfolded the pages as she walked back into the study to wait for Khaled, recognising the handwriting instantly.

Paolo's handwriting.

She wasn't sure whether to be delighted or sad. It was the first letter she'd received from him in all the time she'd been here. Why would he be writing now, unless he was wanting to make amends? She began to read.

Dearest Sapphy,

I realise you may not want to hear from me right now but I could not leave things the unsatisfactory way they were left when last we spoke. For one thing I know I owe you an apology and an expla-

nation and for another, while it may seem melo-
dramatic to you, I continue to fear for your welfare
while you are in Jebbai.

Her lips tightened and she rubbed her forehead. If
Paolo was going to wheel out another bitter diatribe
as to why she should not stay in Jebbai it was going
to fall on deaf ears. Paolo obviously had a problem
with Khaled knowing of his secret marriage. Khaled
must have threatened to reveal the secret long ago—
nothing else would explain why Paolo hated him so
much and wished her to have nothing to do with him.
But she knew the truth now and he would just have
to accept that he had made a mistake by not telling
her. Their whole relationship had been based on a lie.

I realise I owe you a huge apology. I am forever
sorry that I was not the one to tell you of my mar-
riage when I had the chance. I am so afraid the
promise that I made back then to keep my marriage
to Helene a secret has destroyed any chance of
friendship between us in the future. But then, how
could I have told you? I was too scared of losing
you although I wish I'd found a way, as I fear you
must now hate me.

But whatever you think of me, you have to know
the truth, now more than ever.

The circumstances of our marriage were uncon-
ventional to say the least. More relevant to you,
though, my marriage was to a woman promised by
her family and against her will to another and for

that he swore that one day he would have his revenge against me, promising that he would one day steal any woman I intended to marry. And that is why, more than anything, I fear for your safety.

That man was Khaled.

Khaled? Revenge? Her gut clenched and cold tremors assailed her as the impact of Paolo's words hit home. With not a thought to the prospect of creasing the dress, she let herself collapse into an armchair.

So Paolo had married the woman intended for Khaled—no wonder he had a vested interest in revealing Paolo's secret.

But as to his suggestion that Khaled had chosen her because of her links with Paolo… It was crazy. They had never been officially betrothed—unless he had believed the speculation the magazines and gossip columns had spouted…that a link between successful international lawyer, Paolo Mancini, and up-and-coming fashion designer, Sapphy Clemenger, was inevitable.

Was that what she was doing here? Had Khaled lured her here with the promise of a commission in order to 'steal' her from Paolo? It all seemed too incredible. It couldn't be true.

But then, didn't it make more sense than his assertion that he'd fallen in love with her from a photograph and set out to woo her?

She read on, feeling each new revelation like a body blow. Paulo had married Helene to save her from an arranged marriage to Khaled. The arrangement was to be in force only until Khaled found another wife. Then their marriage could be annulled and they would be free to continue with their lives and the relationships they chose. Neither of them expected that twelve years on Khaled would still be waiting, watching, casting the long shadow of his revenge over them.

What kind of bitterness made someone act that way?

No wonder Paolo had been frightened of commitment. No wonder he had pulled away from talk of marriage and the future. He had no choice. Words blurred on the page as tears pricked her eyes at the sacrifice he'd made for a friend, the sacrifice that had cheated him for twelve years of any chance of love.

She blinked the moisture away, clearing her vision enough to allow her to read the final paragraphs.

Sapphy, bella, perhaps I'm wrong. Perhaps the fact that Khaled told you of my marriage is evidence that he's over the past and ready to put it behind him. Maybe it means nothing to him any more. I sincerely hope so.

I know things didn't work out between us and I hope you can start to understand some of the reasons why it was so difficult for me to be honest with you, but I do care for you, Sapphy, I care for you immensely. So please, I beg of you, be careful in your dealings with Khaled. Don't take anything at face value as he has a score to settle with me and I am afraid he will stop at nothing to do it.

Her insides were gutted, totally empty, her heart a black empty chasm pulling wider apart with every breath. Her legs lashed out as she kicked off her heels, reading the paragraphs again, tucking her legs underneath her on the chair, curling tighter and tighter into a ball.

Over the past? Not a chance. Khaled hadn't used his information in the spirit of forgiveness, he hadn't shared it with her over a drink and a laugh for old times' sake. He'd used it as a weapon against Paolo, its barbs designed to dig deep and twist and bury his nemesis completely.

As for stopping at nothing—hadn't he told her he loved her? What was that if not just one more attempt to prevent her leaving and ensure the success of his plan?

She let the pages fall to her lap and hugged herself, her breath jerky, her sobs strangely silent, unable to make a sound because there was absolutely nothing left inside.

Nothing—*except anger.* Into the shell where her heart once resided white-hot anger rushed in on a tidal wave—foaming and crashing, filling the space and gaps, its heat fed with the oxygen from every breath she took.

Khaled had played her for a fool all along. But no longer. Her hands formed into fists and she sprang from the chair, energised by the sudden rush of emotion, letting the pages scatter on the floor.

She had to get this dress off. It was a dress for a bride to wear when she wedded the man of her dreams. She'd been kidding herself that she could ever be that bride. She'd been kidding herself that there would ever be a real wedding. Her dream had turned into a nightmare.

Her hands had tackled only the first of the pearl buttons when behind her someone tapped on the door. She swivelled in time to see the door swing open and suddenly he was there.

'I came as soon...'

With one look at her his words died on his tongue. She was wearing the dress. His blood pumped harder, louder in his veins, spiralling warmth and pride through him. Soon, she would be his.

'Beautiful,' he said, his tone almost worshipping. 'Just stunning. The most beautiful bride ever.'

She sniffed, raising her chin and rubbing her cheek with the back of her hand, and it was then that he noticed her eyes, large and luminescent as if he'd startled her with his sudden appearance, yet smudged around the edges, almost as if she'd been crying.

She dropped her arm to the side and brought herself up taller and suddenly her eyes looked less doe-like and more glacial, and set amongst features that seemed to harden even as he watched.

'Do you think so?' she said, her lips tilting into a harsh curve. She looked down at the dress. 'I was thinking of it more as a going-away outfit.'

'What do you mean?'

She turned her eyes back up at him. Back to where their frosty spears could inflict the most damage. 'When were you going to tell me?'

'Tell you what?'

'Were you going to spring it on me before I'd walked down the aisle, or wait until we were hitched? Or even better, maybe you were saving it for a honeymoon treat?'

'Do you mind telling me what you're talking about?'

'It must have been challenging—always finding ways of keeping me here. But you sure came up with the trump card to beat all today. You love me. Yeah, right. What were you going to try if that didn't work?'

Breath rushed out of his lungs on a growl and he closed the space between them, latching on to her shoulders. 'What's happened?' he said.

'Oh, I get it,' she said, wincing, looking pointedly down on his hands. 'You were planning on physically restraining me. Nice touch. No doubt there's a dungeon somewhere down below where I can be kept for as long as it takes.'

He cursed as he flung his hands from her shoulders, pacing to the desk, where he took two steadying breaths before being able to face her again. 'Something's happened,' he said. 'Are you going to share it with me or are you going to make me stand here and play twenty questions?'

She waved her hand in the direction of the letter, its pages still abandoned in the corner, where they'd fluttered down onto the floor. 'Paolo wrote to me,' she said. 'And it made for interesting reading, the story of your vendetta against him.'

Her eyes glittered blue ice, her chin was set and

defiant and inside he felt sick. This was not the way she should have found out.

He crossed the room, snatching up the pages and scanning their contents.

'This whole trip, my whole reason for being here, was simply so you could satisfy your desire for revenge.'

'It wasn't like that,' he snapped, though he knew it was, at the start.

'Oh? What was it like then? Surely you're not going to tell me you stumbled upon me by accident, completely unaware of my connection with Paolo?

'Oh,' she said, throwing her head back, 'I'm so stupid, I can't believe it's taken me this long to work it all out. You planned this whole fiasco from the start. How convenient that I'm a designer. How easy that proved to be to get me here—all you had to do was pay enough to Gianfranco and he just about pushed me onto you. And once here, you had no intention of letting me go.'

He dragged in a short, sharp breath. 'No! Though it's true I have a score to settle with Paolo.'

'And taking me away from him was part of that vendetta.'

'Why should he have you? He doesn't deserve you. Yes, in the beginning, all I wanted was revenge. But that was before I met you. Then I knew he wasn't good enough for you. That you deserved better.'

'And you were supposed to be better? I believed you, you know. I stood up for you against Paolo when he pleaded with me not to come to Jebbai. I actually felt sorry for your *"fiancée"*, too ill to be able to take part in her own wedding preparations, and yet you were using me the whole time. Using me to get back at him.'

'Maybe it was like that at the start,' he admitted. 'But not all the time. I wanted revenge, that's true, but once I met you I knew you were not just some possession of Paolo's that I had to have. I wanted you for myself then, for the woman you are. I had to have you, body and soul.'

She crossed her arms, the expression on her face mirroring her body language and screaming her disbelief. 'Tell me about Helene,' she said. 'What was so special about her that you couldn't bear the thought of anyone else having her?'

His jaw clenched, teeth grating together. The questions were bound to come, he expected it now, but still that made it no easier to deal with. 'She was young and pretty, a student at university, very clever. Our parents supported the marriage, it would have cemented relations between a huge oil conglomerate and a producing nation. It would have been a good match.'

'Did you love her?'

It was a difficult question and so long ago. He was sure he'd thought he'd loved her once, but now, knowing Sapphire and the way she made him feel— maybe he had just liked the idea of being in love. He shrugged. 'I was barely twenty years old.'

'That doesn't answer my question.'

'Then, no,' he said on a sigh. 'I didn't love her.

But I wanted her. It could have been a good marriage, beneficial to both our families and interests. But it was not to be.'

'Because Paolo got there first.'

'He interfered in something that had nothing to do with him,' he said, his voice rising. 'He should have stayed out of it. And for what he cost me I swore I would take something from him, to make him suffer loss even just a fraction of what I had lost. To make him realise the damage he had done and to make him pay.'

'He saved her! He stepped in and did more than a friend should ever be asked to do, he stood up for her and rescued a terrified girl from a marriage she didn't want, and from a man who would ruin her life. And yet you can't see what an heroic thing he did? Then you pursue him for years, *years*, merely because he snatched something you wanted.'

She paused, her face flushed and eyes wild. 'Don't you think it's time you got over it?'

Breath hissed through his teeth as he sought to bring his breathing under control. 'You think that losing Helene is what this is all about?'

'Isn't it? Though I'm sure your pride took a beating too—knowing that someone was smarter and faster than you. I'm sure you'll never forgive Paolo for that.'

His fist slammed onto the desk, toppling items and scattering pens. Pain shot up his arm but it was nothing compared to the hate. To the pure, unadulterated hate for someone who'd cost him so much.

'That's where you're wrong. I could get over him taking Helene. I could even live with him outsmarting me, if that's how you see it. But I will never forgive him for what he did to my parents.'

'Your parents? What are you talking about?' Her brow furrowed, her head tilting to one side.

'On the day they should have been at my wedding, the day they should have been celebrating my marriage to Helene in London—on that very day, on the side of a Swiss mountain, they were swept away by the avalanche that killed them.'

CHAPTER THIRTEEN

HER hands flew to her mouth, covering a gasp of horror.

'My intended wedding day,' he continued. 'Definitely not a day of joy for anyone. It took the authorities three weeks to recover their bodies and those of their two companions, three weeks where I didn't know whether to hope they would be alive or to hope their bodies would just be found as soon as possible. *Three weeks of hell.*'

She stepped closer, placing her hand on his arm. 'Khaled, I'm so sorry.'

'Are you? Then maybe you understand now why I set out to do what I did. My parents had been in London for the wedding preparations but two days before the bride was spirited away to marry someone else. My mother was distraught, my father embarrassed. There was no point them staying in London to sort out the mess. It wasn't their mess to sort out. My father took her to her favourite resort in an effort to cheer her up, only...'

She squeezed his arm. 'Khaled, I don't know what to say—that's a terrible thing to happen. But you have to realise, it was an accident. You can't blame Paolo.'

'Can't I? Their deaths were the direct consequence of his actions. He didn't just cost me a bride. He cost

166

me my parents. He might as well have killed them himself!' He moved away, just far enough away that she had to let go of his arm.

He didn't want anyone touching him, he felt too raw, just as he had when he'd received the visit from the police, their faces glum, their eyes averted, coming to relate the message from the Swiss authorities that his parents had been swept away and they were doing everything humanly possible to save them.

Just like back then it felt that someone had grated the skin off his body—every part of him felt exposed and raw and weeping.

Her heart was breaking, her anger now tempered with sympathy. It was clear what his parents' deaths had cost him. The young prince had lost his youth, had lost his chance to become his own person before being thrust prematurely into the leadership of the sheikhdom of Jebbai against the backdrop of tragedy.

No wonder he'd focused so much on the circumstances that led to his parents' deaths. No wonder he'd dwelt so much on how he could seek retribution. Paolo was the obvious target.

But his words and the depth of his feeling were shocking. 'Khaled,' she said, 'your parents died in tragic circumstances. But don't let that spoil your whole life. Don't let hate consume you. Don't you think your parents would want you to get on with your life and not dwell on the circumstances of their deaths?'

'You do not understand.'

'I understand that it was fate that took your parents

from you, and had it not been that day it might well have been another. What if the wedding had gone on as planned and they were killed in a motorway accident on their way to the wedding—who would you have blamed then, the bride for agreeing to marry you?'

'That doesn't make sense.'

'Neither does pursuing someone to the ends of the earth for something they had no control over.' He opened his mouth to protest and she launched straight into the next sentence without giving ground. 'Yes, he spoilt your wedding plans, but don't you see, he didn't send your parents to the mountains? It was their choice, you said, to go there. They chose to be on that mountain, not Paolo. You can't blame him for what happened next.'

'And you don't blame your mother for what's happened between you and your sisters?'

His words took her by surprise and she reeled back. 'That's hardly the same thing…'

'Isn't it? She comes back from the dead and now you have competition for your sisters' affections and you don't like it. You actually resent her for being alive. Ironic, isn't it, that I would have given anything for my mother to live and you would be quite happy if your mother had remained safely "dead".'

'Khaled! What a horrible thing to say.'

It wasn't true. It couldn't be true. Sure, she wanted things to be the way they'd always been before, but that was hardly the same thing.

He took a deep breath and dropped his head back.

He felt weary and sick. Heartsick. Was that the word for how it felt when your insides ached as though they'd been pulped?

There was nothing for it now. He had no other means of convincing her to stay, no other words he could say. She'd taken his declaration of love as a lie and why should she suddenly change her mind and believe him now? Attacking her just now would have been the last straw.

'I'm sorry,' he said. 'I should never have said that.' He sighed, long and loud, with the aching tiredness of someone who had hated for far too long. 'I think it's best that I take you to the airport right away. Do you need help packing?'

She looked at him, all wide-eyed and pale, barely moving.

'You have no need to fear. I will not stop you leaving tonight. I'll arrange for the jet and crew to be on standby and send someone to pick up your bags in, say, half an hour?'

This time she nodded, her murmured assent the barest whisper. And then he let himself out of her rooms, letting his eyes drink in until the last click of the door the sight of her in the crumpled gown, committing her sweet lines to memory, knowing that he had forever lost the battle to make her his bride.

They were silent on the way to the airport and for that she was grateful. She doubted she could have spoken anyway, her throat chokingly tight, her chest feeling as if someone had squeezed all the air from it, so there would have been precious little anyway to give sound to her words.

Khaled sat brooding one seat's width and yet an entire world away. He had given up and for that she should be happy. No more lies, no more promises or entreaties. No more declarations of love. She'd thought he might try to convince her that at least that much had been true, that he'd fallen in love with her and that there was still a chance for them, still a future together. She'd been expecting it. She'd even *hoped* that much was true.

But there had been nothing and the emptiness inside her grew as did her certainty that that, too, had been a lie.

At least he was letting her go. Now she could return to Milan; now she would be free.

She looked at the land surrounding the airport road, out over the sandy plains and stunted trees, and her heart ached with the impending separation. So much for being free. Part of her would always belong here, in this desert kingdom with the tall, golden-skinned sheikh named Khaled. With the man she could never now tell she loved.

They passed through airport security, markedly tightened since her arrival, the presence of guards a disturbing but necessary reaction to their earlier troubles. Then they were through the gates and onto the tarmac, where the driver pulled alongside the jet, its engines already warming up. And then her door was being pulled open and before she knew it she was standing at the foot of the steps, Khaled's hands surrounding her own, and the moment had finally come to say goodbye.

She looked up at his face, his jaw set, his dark eyes tortured, and she wanted to kiss his eyes then to kiss away the pain. 'Promise me something,' she said.

His jaw eased up enough for him to speak. 'Promise what?'

'Forget about Paolo. Forget about what happened so long ago. Think about your future, as your parents would want you to do. Can you do that?'

'I'll see,' he said with some effort.

She smiled. It was something at least. 'Thank you.'

'What are your plans?' he asked. 'Will you stay in Milan?'

She exhaled a long breath. 'I don't know. I think I have to go back to Australia first. I need to visit my family. You were right, you know; I've blamed my mother too much for what's happened between my sisters and me. And you've made me realise how lucky I am to have her. I'm going to visit and really get to know her and try to put things right between us.'

He smiled himself then. 'I'm glad. But your work?'

She shrugged. 'Maybe it's time I went out on my own. Gianfranco has been a wonderful teacher, but I'd love to have my own business somewhere…'

She left it there. She didn't need to tell him what kind of shop it would be. Neither of them needed to remember right now what had brought her here or to be reminded of the dress that now lay crushed and tear-stained on her bed.

'I hope you get it,' he said.

'Thank you.'

An officer stepped forward and whispered something in Khaled's ear. He nodded and sighed as the officer stepped back.

'It's time to go, then,' she said, feeling a lump in her throat growing larger and larger.

He nodded. 'It's time.'

'Well, then. Goodbye.'

He looked into her eyes and she saw the swirling emotions that were going on in his and his mouth moved, as if he was on the brink of saying something. And just for a moment she got the impression that he was going to tell her again—tell her that he loved her—and she knew that if he did, then she would tell him too. But then he pressed his lips together and when he did speak it was only to say, 'I'm so sorry.'

He squeezed her hands, bringing her just close enough that he could press his lips to her cheek, lingering there momentarily so she felt for the last time his intake of breath against her skin, the rasp of his five o'clock shadow and the warm sensuality of his lips.

And then he took his mouth away and without looking back at her disappeared into the car.

She shivered. Liquid nitrogen would feel warmer than his cold dismissal. Stiffly she turned and clambered up the stairs, pressing back tears behind a wall of resolve that threatened to tumble at any moment. Through a haze of moisture she was shown to her seat. She tried to smile at the attendant but she didn't know if her face was working. She couldn't feel anything. She was totally numb.

Her eyes searched the windows, looking to catch sight of his car, hoping for a last glimpse of Khaled, but already it was moving towards the security gates, the glass too darkly tinted to see through. He wasn't even waiting for her plane to take off. He'd probably already forgotten her.

The plane's engines whined, doors pulled closed, and gradually, smoothly, it started its taxi to the runway, the security gates slowly disappearing from view as the plane angled away. She craned her head around but it was no good. The gates and the car were gone. She slumped back in her seat, paying scant attention now to the changing view of the airport as a sense of loss like she'd never known weighed down upon her.

What was it worth to be free, when you were leaving your heart behind? What was the point of freedom, when you had lost the one you loved?

That was when she saw it coming. Low and flat, just skimming the roofline over the airport hangars flew the helicopter—perilously close, she thought. But then, it was an airport after all and it could have been coming in to land.

She lost interest momentarily, until her brain registered the danger. It wasn't landing. It was aiming right for them and there was someone hanging on the edge of the door. Something protruding.

A gun!

She gasped as the helicopter drew nearer.

The pilot's voice crackled urgently over the intercom— 'Everyone down!'

She didn't have enough time to be scared, it all happened too fast. Barely had she unbuckled her belt when she was ripped from her seat and thrown bodily to the floor, covered almost completely by the large body of a guard. She was winded but it didn't matter as gunfire battered the side of the aircraft, punching holes through the fuselage and thwacking into the upholstery and fittings around her. Something glass shattered, sending a spray of shards over them both, the guard taking the brunt of the debris.

The engines were still whining, one sounding choppy although the plane had now stopped, and someone was yelling in Arabic. 'What's going on?' she gasped.

The guard above her muttered to her in rough English, 'Stay low; the helicopter is pulling away.' And then suddenly she could breathe again as his weight lifted free.

And all her thought congealed to one certain prospect. Unless the helicopter had decided to melt back into the direction it had come, then it must have found a far more attractive target...

'Khaled!' she screamed, jumping to her feet, knowing that his car would be an easy target from the air, able to be picked out easily on the long, lonely road between the airport and the city.

Then smoke began to fill the cabin, dark and acrid and thick. She was aware of doors opening behind her, of escape chutes being deployed and the wail of sirens as rescue vehicles screamed across the tarmac towards them. Escape was at hand but all she wanted to do was get a quick glimpse to see where the helicopter had gone.

But even as she made for a window someone grabbed her hand, the man who'd covered her earlier, quite possibly saving her life, and pulled her back towards the escape route. Blood trickled from under his hairline and from his hands—the shattered glass—but if he felt his wounds, he gave no indication as he bade her to pull off her low-heeled shoes and quickly mimed the escape routine.

She followed his actions, escaping from the plane and reaching the ground, where already the emergency services were gathered to collect the escaping crew. She was hoisted out of the way and rushed to a vehicle as the cabin crew and security guards followed in rapid order from the smoking jet as sprays from a fire engine began to cover it with foam.

That was when she heard it.

The blast that could only mean an explosion—a mighty boom that came from the direction of the highway. She turned and saw the plume of smoke rising above the desert, black and thunderous and speaking of destruction and death, and something inside her burst open on a silent scream.

Khaled's car!

Her gut clenched in revulsion and panic.

But that would mean…

Khaled—*dead*?

It couldn't be possible. It just couldn't. Not when

she'd never had the chance to tell him what he meant to her. Not when she'd never had the chance to tell him that she loved him.

It didn't matter now, what he'd thought of her. Whether he'd lied to her or not, whether he'd loved her or not, he'd had a right to know that she loved him. What he'd chosen to do with that knowledge should have been up to him, but at least he would have known.

She should have told him that much at least.

She let herself be led into an ambulance. Someone held something to her face and she pulled back but the dressing came away red and she looked at it strangely, wondering that the blood could be hers when she felt no pain but for what had happened to Khaled.

Why were they even bothering with her? Why weren't they looking after him? Hadn't they heard it? Didn't they know?

The ambulance sped away from the plane. 'Where are you taking me?' she asked, hoping desperately that one of them spoke English.

She wasn't disappointed. 'Hebra,' the one who'd held the dressing to her face said. 'Hospital.'

'But what about Khaled?' she begged. 'His car...'

The men looked at each other, exchanging glances that shredded what was left of her heart. Did they know or were they just as scared as she was because they didn't?

They reached the perimeter security gates and stopped. She looked around, wondering about the delay—there was a car blocking their progress, trying to get in. A black car. A black car with two flat tyres, blistered paint and smashed windows.

Khaled's car!

Even as she watched a door opened wide and Khaled jumped out, running to the ambulance as his driver backed the damaged car out of the way.

'Zafeerah?' he shouted, half-demand, half-question, and one of the men nodded and pointed to the rear door. Before she had a chance to lift herself from the stretcher the back doors flew open and Khaled was inside, at her side, hauling her into his arms as the ambulance set off again, its siren screaming, as it sped its way to the city.

Grime stained his golden skin, particles of shattered windscreen lodged in his dark hair, but he was alive—gloriously alive.

'Sapphire,' he said, looking at her, 'I'm so relieved to see you.' He touched his hand to her face. 'But you are hurt.'

She covered his hand with her own, relishing the touch of his strong fingers, feeling his heat replace her earlier chill. Feeling his strength renew her own. She shook her head. 'It's nothing. Your guard saved my life. I don't think I need to go to hospital.'

'You've been through a great deal,' he said. 'You should be looked after properly.'

She felt the tremors start then. Tremors from the shock. From the fear of losing Khaled. From the wave of relief on discovering he was alive. He held her tight, rocking her, soothing her fears.

'I was so scared,' he said. 'When I heard the helicopter fire on the jet, I was so damned scared. But you are safe.' He hugged her closer, burying his face into her hair. 'I cannot believe it.'

His lips brushed kisses over her forehead, down the line of her nose.

'I heard the explosion,' she said, her fingers clutching his shirt. 'And I—' She broke off, her voice cracking. 'I was so afraid.'

Something shifted in his eyes, peeling away a layer so that something below shone through, burnished like copper lights, alive with hope.

'The helicopter. It came in close but by then it was already too late. A mortar from the airport guards brought it down. It crashed alongside the road.'

She swallowed. It must have been close, for the car's paint to be blistered with the heat, the tyres all but melted from the rims. She squeezed her eyes shut, trying to banish those pictures. They didn't matter now. Not with Khaled alive, holding her.

'I saw the pilot,' he said. 'I recognised her.'

'Her? Who was it?'

'Azizah.'

She gasped, unable to grasp the concept of her meek servant being capable of committing acts of terrorism. 'I can't believe it. She was so sweet, so helpful.'

He sighed deeply, shaking his head. 'Saleem began to suspect something was not right and he tried to tell me to get rid of her because he was worried for your safety. But I didn't listen. She came from a good family, with a long and loyal history with the palace. I could not believe she would betray us. By the time we had discovered the truth, she had fled.'

Saleem had been concerned for her welfare? And yet she had been so suspicious of him, so afraid of the way he watched her and of his abrupt manner. It was Azizah—timid, shy Azizah—who'd been the real danger. How she had made a mess of everything.

'But why?' she asked. 'What did she have against you?'

'Her parents were my parents' closest aides. It was they who died along with my parents in the avalanche. Azizah was only five years old at the time. We paid a pension and for her upbringing, it was the only thing we could do, and relatives in Jamalbad brought her up. But it seems they never forgave me for what had happened to their family and their hatred fed into her for twelve years until she became their vehicle for retribution.'

He hugged her closer. 'I cannot believe I entrusted you to such a dangerous woman. Can you ever forgive me?'

She shivered, wondering how much further the bitter tentacles of revenge could reach. There had to be an end to the pain, to the anguish. Somewhere the cycle had to be broken.

'I'm so sorry,' he whispered and she trembled again, remembering the last time he had used that expression.

'Do you still want me to leave?' she asked, her voice soft and uncertain.

'What do you mean? You're going straight to hospital.'

'I mean afterwards. The last time you told me you were sorry, you put me on the plane and walked away.' She swallowed deeply, trying to force down the fear of revealing the truth, steeling herself to go on because she knew she had no choice. 'Because if that's what you still want, I'll live with it, but there's something I must tell you first.'

His brows pulled together, his eyes unsure. 'I thought you wanted to leave. I thought you couldn't wait to see the back of me.'

'At one time that was true, but not for the reason you might think.'

'Then why?'

'Because I was scared of the way you made me feel. From the start I felt an attraction to you. Even when I knew I shouldn't. Even though I knew you were marrying someone else. I knew that if I stayed too long then I wouldn't want to leave. I knew that the longer I stayed, the more I came to know you, then the more I was in danger of falling in love with you.'

Silence stretched out between them, tension and expectation heightening against the backdrop of the wailing siren, and she feared she'd already said too much.

'And?' he prompted at last. He sounded impatient, giving her a kernel of hope. Did he really care what she had to say? Would it make a difference?

'And it happened. I didn't want it to. I even tried

to fight it. But it was no good. There was nothing I could do to stop it. Then when the jet was attacked and I feared for your life, I knew I was wrong not to have told you.'

'Hold on,' he said, holding a finger to her lips. 'Take a deep breath. What should you have told me?'

She blinked and sucked in a lungful of air, hoping for a burst of courage to go with it. 'I love you, Khaled. Somewhere along the way, in the midst of all that has happened, I fell in love with you.'

'You did?' He looked as if he didn't quite believe her.

She nodded. 'My pride wouldn't let me tell you. I was still so angry about everything that had happened. But pride and anger are such worthless emotions when so much is at stake. When I thought you'd been attacked and I feared for your life, I knew then that even if you never loved me in return, if you survived, I needed to let you know the truth. I needed to be honest with you.'

'But I don't understand. What do you mean, if I never loved you? I *told* you I loved you. You knew that.'

She gazed up at him. 'I thought you only said that to prevent me from leaving.'

'No.' He touched the tip of her nose with one finger. 'I told you that because I loved you.'

'But that was before I opened Paolo's letter. You never once told me after that—when we argued and you said you'd take me to the airport—you never mentioned it. You made me think it was just another ploy, another tactic to keep me here.'

'Not a ploy.' He gave a sad smile. 'But I understand why you would think so. I have never treated anyone as badly as I have treated you.'

She opened her mouth to protest—there were reasons why he acted the way he did, she knew that now. But two fingers on her lips shushed her.

'I cannot ask for forgiveness, it is too much. I planned to cold-heartedly steal you from one man and take you for my own—'

'No, Khaled, don't.' She brushed his hand aside, only to have him muffle her objections with his kiss.

'Please, let me explain,' he said, finally lifting his lips from hers, asserting his will instead with his dark eyes. 'I need to tell you these things. If you can bear to hear them.'

Her teeth scraped her bottom lip. She'd told him she loved him and he'd confirmed that he loved her. She wasn't sure she wanted to hear any more, certainly not if that risked changing the balance, but she nodded anyway. There must be no more secrets. Just as he needed to tell her these things, she needed to hear them.

'At first I set out to have you because of Paolo, that much is true. I had seen photos, I knew you were attractive and successful, but I had no doubt I could bend you to my will and make you go along with my plan. A month would be all I'd need.'

He took a deep breath. 'But from the moment I met you, my plan was in trouble. I began to want you, right from the start, and not just because you belonged to someone else. It was almost as if there was something between us—a wire—invisible and tightly strung, that pulled tighter and tighter the longer we were together.'

'I felt it too,' she offered. 'I couldn't get you out of my head, even when I thought I was designing a wedding dress for another woman—another bride.'

'You did? Of course, I suspected as much.' His smile turned suddenly serious. 'But still, the way I treated you was inexcusable. Even though I couldn't get enough of you. It was the ultimate irony that the woman I had stolen to get back at another man had gone and stolen my heart.'

He sighed. 'You made me risk the entire plan by telling you two weeks early.'

'I did that?'

He nodded. 'Believe it. You needled and bullied and refused to give in to my excuses for not having a fitting. You drove me so crazy with your demands that I wanted to throw you off balance.' He smiled. 'And I did,' he said, earning him a quick punch in the arm.

'I thought you were mad,' she said.

'It was a form of madness,' he agreed. 'I was so mad for you. And when you said you were going home to Paolo, I just got madder still. How could you prefer him over me?

'And if the airport hadn't been closed yesterday, I would have let you go home then, so deep did you seem affected by the pain of betrayal. Except…'

He paused and she waited expectantly.

'Except what?'

'Except, even then...' his voice sounded tenser, more strung out '...even then the drive for revenge was so strong. I knew that if you came to me of your own free will then my revenge on Paolo would be that much sweeter.'

'If I came to you of my own free will...' Her thoughts shifted her back to the desert tent, where she'd been the one to initiate lovemaking. She'd been the one to make the decision. The one to decide. She could have let him pull away from his kiss and leave the tent but no, she'd been the one to take that fateful step.

'I told you—I've treated you so badly.'

'And I have something to tell you.' She looped her arms around his neck. 'Paolo and I weren't getting married. Certainly not lately and neither, I believe, in the future.'

'But—'

'I know,' she said, 'we were touted as the next great love interest and for a time there I thought that's where we were headed, and while it hurt—*a lot*—that he'd never told me he already had a wife, us getting married wouldn't have happened, whether or not you intervened. He'll always be a good friend but he just wasn't the one.'

He looked at her strangely. 'You mean, after all my planning, I still didn't get to steal Paolo's bride?'

She shook her head. 'No. Does that mean you need

to go steal someone else to satisfy your need for revenge?'

'No.' He broke into a broad grin. 'I ended up with something much better than revenge. I ended up with you.'

'Oh, I love you, Khaled,' she said, pulling him close. 'I love you more than you could ever know.'

He pushed her away and for a moment she resisted. Until she saw his eyes and the love that shone there, deep and true.

'You do? After everything that has happened?'

She nodded, exhilarated at having the truth revealed at last—all of it. 'And things will be different from now on. No more talk of revenge and retribution. The past is gone and buried. From now on it will be love that drives the future.'

'Oh, yes,' he said, 'love for you, my dazzling Sapphire; love between us.'

He broke off the kiss that followed suddenly— much too suddenly, confusing her with his sudden withdrawal. She blinked her eyes open to find his studying hers, their darkness bright with excitement.

'You would not have to give up your work if you stay,' he said, his words coming almost too fast for her to keep up with. 'You mentioned you wanted your own salon. Would you consider having one here, in Hebra?'

She drew in a breath. She hadn't thought about it, hadn't thought through the ramifications of revealing her love, the thrill of finding it reciprocated, the surprise that he wouldn't expect her to give up the career she loved.

But why not Hebra? It was time she branched out on her own and there was nothing now to tie her to Milan. From what she'd learnt, Hebra was a thriving city, its women as proud and as fashion conscious as any in Paris or Milan.

She started nodding, her excitement building, thinking of the stock still in the workroom at the palace and the excellent seamstresses she knew were available. It would be almost too easy.

And it was almost too much to take in—the prospect of having both her own salon and the love of the man beside her. Who said you couldn't have it all?

She smiled and kept on nodding. 'It could work, yes.'

'I knew it!' His words exploded from him in a rush. 'Then so be it. You shall have your own salon and your designs will be world famous.'

'I don't need to be world famous,' she said as his lips moved closer to hers, 'so long as I have your love.'

His mouth turned into a smile, the darkness of his eyes melting to warm velvet. 'Oh, you have my love. You hold my heart and soul forever.'

Sheer bliss welled up inside as his mouth slanted across hers and he kissed her, slowly, languorously, thoroughly, in both a confirmation and a celebration of their love. Finally he drew back his head. 'After all that's happened, I wonder—is this too soon to ask you if you'd do me the honour of becoming my wife?'

'It's not too soon at all,' she answered, unable to restrain the bubbling joy from her voice. 'So why don't you go ahead and ask me?'

He smiled and then his eyes glittered and the smile dropped away to something entirely more purposeful. 'Marry me, Sapphire. Make me the happiest and luckiest man in the world by agreeing to become my wife.'

'Yes,' she said, 'I will marry you!' her laughter welling up with love and certainty, her face pressed brow to brow against his as his lips closed in for another kiss.

'After all, I already have the perfect dress.'

The Arranged Brides

Settling a score—and winning a wife!

If you enjoyed STOLEN BY THE SHEIKH,
don't miss the second book in the fan-favorite author
Trish Morey's brand-new duet.

THE MANCINI
MARRIAGE BARGAIN
On sale in March

Paolo Mancini married Helene Grainger to save her
from a forced marriage—twelve years on he's back, to
tell her they can divorce. But Paolo is still the gorgeous
Italian Helene married. Now they are reunited, and he
has no intention of letting his wife go....

Find out how the story unfolds.

Available wherever books are sold.

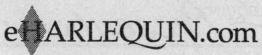

uNcut

Even more passion for your reading pleasure!

Escape into a world of passion and romance!

You'll find the drama, the emotion, the international
settings and happy endings that you love in Presents.
But we've turned up the thermostat a little, so that the
relationships really sizzle.... Careful, they're almost
too hot to handle!

**Check out the first book in this
brand-new miniseries....**

Cameron Knight is on a dangerous mission when
he rescues Leanna.

THE DESERT VIRGIN,
by Sandra Marton

on sale this March.

"*The Desert Virgin* has it all from thrills to danger
to romance to passion."
—Shannon Short, *Romantic Times BOOKclub* reviewer

Look out for two more thrilling Knight Brothers stories,
coming in May and July!

www.eHarlequin.com   HPUC0306

If you enjoyed what you just read,
then we've got an offer you can't resist!

Take 2 bestselling love stories FREE!

Plus get a FREE surprise gift!